Friendzzz

13 Short Stories on
Friendship

VIKAS JAURIHAR

INDIA · SINGAPORE · MALAYSIA

ISBN 979-8-89026-373-5

Contents

Introduction

The entire script is a work of fiction that is not intended to resemble any special person in my life or anyone close to me. It is a mix of imagination and understanding of the dynamics of friendship that could be easily observed when you have been through it.

The book speaks about the relationship that we chose according to our wish i.e. friendship. Friends bring smiles to our faces. However hard our journey is, their companionship makes the path easier. Friends never leaves us in a bad time. Pals are the ones who cheer and motivate us when the chips are down. People who had friends for a lifetime are quite lucky as they have someone special in life with whom they can share all their sorrows and happiness. It is a different story whether we were able to maintain the relationship with our friends or not in the long run. All the chapters show different types of pals and a few might reciprocate with a few readers who had led similar lives.

As an author, this is my first try, at a story based on friendship. It has been a very fulfilling experience as I walked down memory lane while narrating the entire episodes of book. I have kept it simple so that as a reader you relate to the same easily.

Introduction

I would be really happy even if a single reader could reminisce about their golden days when they spent a lively childhood with their comrades.

It was a bit difficult writing this book as I am a working professional and so my only priority now is to grow on the corporate ladder. The decision of penning this book was crucial for me to come out of the monotony of a 10 am-7 pm job. I thoroughly enjoyed writing this book and hope all my readers would love it too.

I would like to thank my wife, mother, sisters, and all my friends who guided me in completing this book in a short period.

Twist

It was Naveen's first day in college and he wanted to look cool. He was dressed in a white floral shirt with blue denim. Knowingly he has worn this as he knew that he always receives compliments on this deadly combination (back at his home and school). This is what he thought or perceived but to his dismay, nobody was observing him, not even the peon in the college. A kind of loneliness engulfed his mind and he started feeling out of place. He was used to being the center of attraction among his friends for his great sense of humor and dashing looks but now at the institution, he was feeling isolated and depressed. The class was brimming with students. He maintained a low profile and sat in the front row meaningfully with the hope that somebody might join him but to his shock, most of the students were busy among themselves as they knew each other (probably because they were local) but he was unacquainted with any of them (as he was from a different city).

Half an hour passed by, and his anxiousness grew to the next level. He started praying to God to send some angels to overcome boredom and desolation. He kept his eyes closed praying and then some miracle happened. It was as if God has listened to his desperate calls. A very sweet voice broke his forced meditation.

Unknown: Hello, can I sit here?

Naveen: (Opening his eyes) Of course, why not?

Unknown: Hi, my name is Sneha and I belong to Jabalpur.

Naveen: Oh great, I am too an outsider and for me this town is new. And you know I am feeling very low today as I have a habit of being surrounded by friends but here, see nobody cares for others. I have been sitting here for the last 30 minutes and not a single person approached me for friendship. Is it the right way to treat an outsider? No, God forbid if something happens to me, nobody out here will come to help me.

And he went on questioning and answering all by himself for another 15 minutes.

Finally, breaking the chord, she hesitantly asked.

Sneha: By the way what is your name?

Naveen: Oh, so sorry, I just forgot to introduce myself. My name is Naveen and I belong to Ranchi.

Sneha: Ok. Nice name. It seems you have created lots and lots of expectations from the college and people around here. Let me give you just one piece of advice, just take things as it comes, and don't worry as in a few days things would change. Also, if people do not approach you, then go ahead and introduce yourself. Magic will happen.

Naveen stared at Sneha as if she has spoken something out of the world but then controlled himself, in a very low tone, almost in a whisper uttered.

Naveen: Do you follow some monk or what?

Sneha: Why?

Naveen: Your lecture seemed more like a sermon. That is why.

Sneha could not control her laughter with the way Naveen blurted those funny lines (along with a tone of innocence that was quite palpable in his voice).

Well now the two had become friends and every day they would spend time together in off-hours after college. Surprisingly, both were very lean and thin. They called each other by nicknames 'patlu' and 'patli' respectively which means skinny in the Hindi language.

Time passed by slowly, and eventually, they made a few more friends. Their group grew to 6-7 people who were always ready to play some kind of mischief or pranks. Sometimes they would bunk the classes and go to watch movies or restaurants to have lunch/dinner. Sneha would often pay Naveen's bills as he would always have an empty wallet (he used to spend all his money on dresses as he had an affinity for the same). Sometimes Sneha would get irritated as many times he would ask her to join him for lunch or dinner and post-meal, at the restaurant he would shamelessly divulge that he does not have money. Well, that is why she would always keep extra bugs with herself as she never trusted him, especially for finances. She would laugh it off most of the time as she knew that Naveen is one such pampered child who does not like to take responsibility.

Sneha was always big emotional support for Naveen as whenever he was tense, he would come down to her for suggestions. He believed that she is the right person who gives the right advice without any prejudices and biases.

On the other hand, Sneha was dependent on Naveen for her studies as he was more studious. He would help her, especially in Mathematics and Chemistry which she found a bit difficult to understand. One fine day when Naveen went to meet Sneha in her hostel, he found her to be severely ill. Her body temperature was quite high around 104 degrees. Her face has turned pale and it seemed she would faint anytime out of weakness. Immediately he took her to the hospital where she was admitted and saline dips were injected into her body. After 24 hours her temperature dropped down. On proper diagnosis, it was found that she was suffering from 'Jaundice.' Her parents could not come as they both were suffering from high BP and sugar. Their family doctors had strictly recommended they not make any kind of travel plans. Now for the first time in his life, Naveen faced a situation where he was to take complete responsibility and control of the situation. But he did that fantastically with complete devotion. He took care of Sneha very nicely, stayed 2 nights at the hospital, on daily basis brought fruits for her consumption, and made sure that she does not miss her parents' presence. Slowly and gradually, she recovered but it took a great toll on her studies. The exams were approaching and her preparations were incomplete. In this sphere also Naveen took the charge and for the next 10 days, he went to her hostel for joint studies where he helped her in grasping the chapters as much as possible. Sneha had never imagined that Naveen could be so accountable ever in his life.

Sneha: Naveen, it seems you have grown up.

Naveen: Hello, what do you mean by this? My parents say I am the most responsible person on earth.

Sneha: Really! Was that the joke of the year?

Naveen could not control his smile and Sneha too burst into laughter.

Three years passed by and very soon the time came when they had to leave the college after completion of the final academic session. Naveen wanted to appear for the public service exam and Neha was more interested in the fashion world. So as per choices, they both tread different paths. For the next three long years, they were not in touch with each other.

Naveen had cracked both the written & Viva exam of IAS and got posted in one of the towns as a sub-divisional magistrate (he has fulfilled the first & foremost goal of his life). Throughout his journey, he had toiled hard for this moment but now after attaining it, he wanted to chill and relax a bit. The first thing that came to his mind was to get the whereabouts of Sneha. He scanned all digital media space to get any information about her but every time he failed miserably. He was quite amazed as Sneha was a very socially active girl and always loved to make her presence feel in all kinds of public groups. (Suddenly vanished from all limelight without any trace or hint was a bit of concern for him). Naveen did not lose hope, rather he started calling all his college friends to find out any piece of news about her. Finally got the information from one of their very old common friends Ruchi. She communicated to him that Sneha had set up a boutique in the picturesque solitary town but she prefers to live a life of seclusion away from the noisy city life. Though he could not understand the reason for such a private life. But without giving a single thought, he then immediately planned and left for the place where she was based (He had applied for 2 days' leave from the office due to personal reasons).

He reached the town and then the store at around 6 pm. Sneha was addressing a customer explaining to her the kind of materials that were used in a particular piece of dress. He patiently waited for the client to leave. Once the customer had left, he hastily rushed towards her.

Naveen: Excuse me, can you show me some kind of trendy outfit for me?

Sneha: (Without raising her head) Sorry Sir, we only cater to women as this is an exclusive ladies' store.

Naveen: Sorry, by 'me' I meant a dress for a friend who is a girl.

Sneha: (Slightly raising her head) Sir, what kind of dress would you prefer?

Seeing Naveen standing in front of her, for a second, she got dumbstruck. Not able to utter a single word, all she could do was just keep staring at him in disbelief. Naveen broke the silence.

Naveen: Sneha, so mean of you. See I covered 300 kilometers to meet you and you are giving me such a cold & blank welcome to me.

Sneha: (Controlling all her emotions) Nothing like that Naveen, it is just that clients are around. Can we go to the coffee shop which is just around the corner? Just give me 15 minutes.

Naveen: Sure, take your time.

Naveen was not able to understand how could Sneha behave in such a weird manner as during their college days she used to be a chirpy girl. Now he could see a very sober woman who has changed a lot in the last few years.

Soon after handing over the keys to one of her staff, she came out of the shop.

Sneha: Sorry Naveen, hope you didn't mind waiting for me.

Naveen: Come on, during my college days I do not remember how many times you had kept me waiting. It was infinite as I could not count it.

Sneha smiled and finally, he could see some sort of happiness on her face. They reached the coffee shop and ordered two cups of cappuccino.

Naveen: Sneha, you have changed a lot.

Sneha: What makes you say so?

Naveen: Look at yourself. Your face used to glow during college time and it was you who taught me to laugh at myself. But now I only see the shadow of despair and sadness on your look. What has happened to you girl?

Sneha: I lost my mom and dad last year in a car accident, Naveen.

Her face has turned whitish and it seemed she wanted to cry her heart out in front of her friend. But she remained as hard as a rock and not a single drop of tear rolled down her eye. She stood frozen like ice, expressionless and cold.

This left Naveen more worried as he never imagined that he would meet Sneha in such a depleted condition. Sneha was the single child of her parent and had no siblings, thus there was a complete lack of emotional support in her life. Naveen was very much aware of it. He had decided that he will not let Sneha suffer anymore but was quite confused as to what he should do now. Finally, he took charge of the situation and after having the coffee ordered like a guardian.

Naveen: Sneha today I would prepare the dinner for you.

Sneha: (Jokingly) I do not want to die so young.

Naveen: Listen, famous personalities have tasted food prepared by me and they all gave me personal compliments for the heavenly pleasure that I gave to their taste buds. Now just take me to your house.

Sneha: Ok, would take you along with me provided we share the food preparation. You make the chicken curry and the rest of the things I would cook. Is this condition acceptable to you?

Naveen: Absolutely Madam.

Both reached Sneha's house and Naveen quickly made the first move by taking the initiative of readying the food assigned to him. Once he was done preparing the food, he let his guard down and called Sneha to make the rest of the dishes. Meanwhile, he opened the TV to watch the live cricket match to loosen up. But he was feeling restless as he was not able to digest the gloomy, low-spirited, and depressed Sneha. Suddenly, his eyes fell on the red diary that caught his attention. It was lying beside the table lamp. He immediately recognized the same as it was the same notebook that Sneha used to carry in her college days. She had a habit of noting down all the daily details in it as a routine and was very possessive about it. Nobody dared to touch it as she would pounce up on anyone like a wild cat if anyone tried to have a look at it.

Naveen was curious and even though he comprehended that it was uncalled for to check someone's diary, he picked up the notebook and started reading it. The first 100 pages had all the childhood memories inscribed on them. He wanted to unwrap their college days' stories and thus he started overlapping the pages hastily. Very soon he came across the sheet where the details of the college section had started.

"My first day in college and I made a new friend whose name is Naveen. He seems to be a gentle guy but is a bit obnoxious and likes boasting about himself. Good thing is that even though I was feeling lonely, I never told him. He gave me great companionship at least on the first day. Thank God.

He continued reading and after a few more pages, he noticed in one of the sheets where she has mentioned her birthday celebration.

"Today was my birthday and Naveen made me feel special. He arranged a small get-together for all my close friends and then gifted me a wristwatch. Thanks to him and all my dear friends for such a lovely day."

Suddenly Sneha screamed and Naveen ran towards the kitchen to see what made her do so.

Naveen: What happened Sneha? Are you all, right?

Sneha: No, I am not all right. Can't you see that fearsome ugly lizard licking out its tongue horribly as if it is inviting me for a dual fight?

Naveen: Come on Sneha. I did not know that you are so fragile that a small reptile can scare the hell out of you.

Naveen used a small broom to weed off the lizard and then returned to the drawing room to complete the unfinished diary. He re-opened the page from where he has left and very soon reached the leaf which created a storm in his life. In one of the sheets, there was something that rattled his heart and mind forever.

"Today I returned from the hospital after 7 days of hospitalization. I am alive because of Naveen as he took care of me in this adverse moment of my life. I think I like him, rather I am sure that I love him. But I do not want to break our friendly relationship by sharing my feelings with him. Period. If something must happen, it will happen naturally".

His head started swinging and for a minute he sat there like a statue. A deafening sound of lightning outside finally broke his thoughtfulness. He felt an acute pain in his head but then he somehow gathered himself and rolled down on the bed. Meanwhile, Sneha readied the food and came out to check on Naveen. By then he has placed the diary in the same place and position so that it looks untouched.

Sneha: Wow, so you are having a nice time. I am so tired Naveen, after a long gap I have made so many recipes at a stretch, two vegetable curry, rice, roti, pulses, salads, etc. Generally, when I am alone, I prefer plain food.

Naveen was quiet but he knew that he needs to behave normally, otherwise she would get a kind of hint that something is wrong.

Both had dinner together and again shared some lighter moments. Naveen gave his best to not show any kind of expression or emotions there that could create doubts in Sneha's mind. Post dinner, he left for his hotel but continuously all memories of the past kept flashing in his mind. The entire night he could not sleep well as the aggrieved and distressed face of Sneha incessantly revolved around his wide-open eyes.

The next morning, he was clear as to what he needed to do. He called up Sneha.

Naveen: Sneha, I want to meet you again.

Sneha: What happened Naveen, it is just that yesterday we met, and now once again you want to see me. Mister, what is your intention?

Naveen: Nothing as such Mother India. Just wanted to convey something before I leave the town.

Sneha: Ok, come at 7 pm. I would be free by then.

Naveen: Ok mam.

Naveen was a bit chilled out that day, went to a saloon, had a haircut, bought a new informal shirt for himself, and waited for the evening to arrive. Sharp at 6 pm, he left for Sneha's place. On the way, he bought a bunch of roses, a lovely gown for her, and a packet of Cadbury. He had called her at the same coffee shop where they had met yesterday. By 7:30 pm, Sneha was there at the outlet.

Naveen: Hi Sneha.

Sneha: Wow! For the first time, you are looking so well dressed and groomed. What is the matter, boss?

Naveen: Come on you could have complimented me by saying that I look handsome, instead of that you find pleasure in taunting me. So, mean of you, girl.

Sneha: Ok. I am sorry. But I mean it. You are looking like a stud.

Naveen: Thank You. Thank You. (He said with excitement)

The next moment, Naveen took out the rose bouquet from his bag and handed it to Sneha. Sneha was too flabbergasted to see the gesture.

Sneha: What is this for Naveen?

Naveen: Wait, wait. I have a few more things to offer.

One by one he presented the dress and then the chocolate to the lady. Sneha was awestruck as she was not used to such kind of attention.

Naveen: Did you like it?

Sneha: Yes of course and I do not know how to share it but yes, I am on top of the world today.

Saying this tears started rolling down her cheek. She cried there for another half an hour inconsolably. This is what Naveen wanted as somewhere in between the thread of life, she had been trying hard to keep her emotions intact to herself and this had created a lot of stress in her mind. Naveen too was overwhelmed as he knew that he cannot reciprocate the love Sneha has for him but yes, he can show his affection for her by other means, the sample of which he has done today. He also shared an envelope with her which had a handwritten letter by him addressed to her and pressed her to go through it when she is alone, at least not in front of him.

In the night when Sneha was all alone, she read the letter.

Dear Sneha,

"In the tiny voyage of life, you want to remain associated with people who become an essential part of your world. I without an iota of doubt can say that you are one such person who would always remain special in my heart. No matter how strong the hurricane is, I would always be there for you, to stand against all odds and difficulties. I know while reading this sheet, your eyes would be filled with a tear, but don't cry as I will always try my best to spread layers of happiness in your life.

Just want to keep you updated that just one month back I got engaged to a girl who has been selected by my parents. The marriage would happen a month later, so please consider this as an informal invitation from my end, and very soon would come in person to invite you.

You would be surprised as to why I am sharing this all via a letter. Sneha, you know me very well, though I am a chatterbox but feel shy sharing personal feelings openly, so I thought of expressing myself with a handwritten note which, if you want, can frame, and preserve forever. Just kidding.

Take care and will meet you soon."

Your Naveen.

Sneha for a second was stunned as she could not understand what to do. But once again she cried her heart out at the same moment. She had a kind of feeling as if a part of her life has departed from her forever. Eventually, it gave her more courage as she knew that she will have to stride her path unaided all alone herself now and should detach from any unwanted expectations. All these years she knowingly did not connect with Naveen as she was aware that she may fall in love with him all over again. But as a human sometimes we become powerless as no one is stronger than destiny. Naveen came searching for her which she least expected. One thing, that gave her immense satisfaction, was that her old friend is now part of her life and their friendship remained unharmed. Any wrong step by her could have crumbled their beautiful bond and relationship.

!!!

Fight

Sanjay had scored good marks in his 10th board examination with above distinction percentile in science and Mathematics (both were his favorite). He aspired to become an engineer, so he always used to put extra effort into these subjects. His father was a mechanical engineer in a reputed organization who always wanted the best education for his son. He believed in his son's ability and knew that he could do wonders if guided well in his academics. Sanjay was too shy and never felt comfortable in and around strangers. For him, life has never been an easy journey as he lost his mother at an early age. This directly impacted his personality making him quite an introvert. He found solace in staying alone and avoided active social life. The only passion that he carried was to crack the joint engineering entrance exam and get inducted into a premium institute in the country. Thus, he had earmarked Kendriya Vidyalaya school for higher secondary education (+2) which boasts of highly qualified teachers in the nation. It had a C.B.S.E curriculum that closely follows the syllabus and pattern of the JEE (that can act as a stepping stone towards his dream of studying at a top-notch engineering university).

Sanjay had submitted all his 10th standard certificates and filled the admission form due diligently so that it remains error-free. Luck was on his side as the very next week he received a call to join the school, the session was going to start soon. Just a day before joining the same, he went to a nearby temple along with his family to pray for the well-being of himself and his near & dear ones. The next morning was supposed to be his first day in the institution, so he woke up early, readied himself, and got on the bus. The absolute distance of the same was 10 Km from his home.

Adjusting to a completely new environment always turned out to be a unique experience for Sanjay. This would be the third time when he needs to adjust to a new place. The first was when his father got transferred to a place called Neyveli, in Tamil Nadu. The second was when the family shifted to a small town in Orissa. All those initial changes had made him mentally strong and accommodating. The first day always brings in unique moments. As usual like his nature, it was an awkward moment for him as he was surrounded by new faces, for a second, he felt out of place but then gathered all his positive energies. He cannot quit his dreams for any unknown reason or fear.

The school was very beautiful, with walls painted in an eye-catchy blue and white color, with pictures of great freedom fighters incorporated on it vividly. There was lots of greenery inside the campus. It had two huge grounds with lots of space for different games like Volleyball, cricket, and football. He was quite happy to see it as he loved playing games. It gave him a kind of goosebumps, his first impression was mind-blowing, just beyond his expectation. His anticipation grew multifold and he patted himself for making the very right decision in his life.

He walked quietly towards the class deeply engrossed in profound thoughts, looking keenly at every feature and landmark of the place. He got so lost in it, that for a minute got clueless as to which lane would lead to his class. He had just once visited his class before when he had come down to the school to submit his admission form and mark sheet. As he was getting late, so he got hold of a younger kid passing by and asked him.

Sanjay: Where is the Standard 11 science class?

Kid: Go straight and then take a right cut in the end, post that walks 50 meters straight, then turn left. The first class on turning to your left lies your class.

Sanjay: Thank you, dear.

As instructed by the kid, he went straight, took a right cut, and then walked 50 meters & turned left. To his surprise, he found the boy's toilet in front of him (Moment of Truth). He wanted to abuse that kid badly but he was nowhere to be seen around. Now he decided not to trust anyone and find the class all by himself. He was panicking a bit but then controlled his nerves as he did not want his freaking looks to be seen by anyone. Here and there, he wasted a lot of time, meanwhile, the morning assembly school gathering bell rang and he saw students coming out of their classes in a queue walking towards the meeting ground for morning prayer. Breaking his pledge, he hurriedly asked the peon whom he saw standing nearby for the right location. To his utter surprise without asking a single question to him, the person took him to the room where he met his classmates for the first time. All the students were staring at him as if he belongs to a different planet. His was a new face, the rest of the entire students were from the same school (they all had passed 10th from the same institution), only he being the fresh joiner. They too were in the process of forming the line to attend the assembly prayer on the ground. A batchmate named Anubhav walked toward him.

Anubhav: Hi, from which school have you joined and why?

Sanjay: My previous school's name was St. Joseph and I wanted to be part of this dynamic school that has a very good set of teachers.

Anubhav: Who told you that we have teachers?

Sanjay: What do you mean? Don't we have them?

Anubhav: Oh, yes, we have but the chemistry teacher has been on sick leave for the last two months, that is before our session started, till date she has not joined back. Our prescribed Mathematics teacher position is vacant and we have been assigned a junior teacher for the same. The English teacher explains the subject in a Shakespearean language that is understood by none of us.

Sanjay's face turned pale on hearing this. He was about to ask further questions but Anubhav stopped him saying that let's complete our morning prayers first and then we could discuss it further.

Post the assembly, the entire batch returned to the classroom. The first class was Physics and a very fair tall handsome teacher entered the class. All the students stood up and greeted the lecturer.

Lecturer: Good morning to all. Today we will cover our first chapter 'Law of Motion' but before that let us all get familiarized with each other. So, one by one please get up and introduce yourself. Also, share the reason for taking science as your primary subject.

It was quite fun as the answers of a few students were amusing like "I took science because my parents insisted, I do the same". Some said, "I did not have any other option as Arts and Commerce subjects are not my cups of tea". Few said, "It will enable them to achieve greater success in the future and enlighten their career". Out of all, one answer stood out, uttered by none other than Naushad. He said, "I took science because I love Physics and, in the future, I would like to do some research work". The kind of clarity the boy had in his voice and thoughts, attracted a lot of attention. Naushad was a studious, flamboyant, and fine-looking guy who was a favorite of all teachers due to his knowledge, etiquette, and well manners. All in all, he was a complete package and everyone in the class liked him.

Sanjay took note of it as he believed that in the company of good people, he too will get inspiration to do better in life. So, he made the first step in initiating the interaction with Naushad. Keeping aside all his inhibitions, he walked to present himself to the intelligent guy.

Sanjay: Hi Naushad, my name is Sanjay and as you know I am a new joiner in the class.

Naushad: Nice meeting you Sanjay. Welcome to our school. Well, feel at ease and if you require any help, do let me know.

Sanjay: Well can you make me a scholarly student like you? (There was a seriousness in his tone).

Naushad: (With a sweet but naughty smile on his face) I do not manufacture intellectual people. But I think I should start doing so as I have a few more pending requests.

Sanjay and Naushad laughed out loud. From there on their friendship started nurturing. They sat on the same bench in the class and during their free hours they would spend time together chatting with each other. There were a few funny incidents that happened in their lives in the school.

The first one was the unit test in which the questions of Physics given to them were very tough. Sanjay was panicking as he saw a few words on the question sheet which he had never heard of, so out of helplessness, he asked his friend to show him the answers. He just wanted a passing mark, well Naushad assured him not to worry as he knows the answer and once, he has completed it, he would show him the paper. Sanjay kept on waiting but was losing his patience as the time was running out. Once again, he requested Naushad.

Sanjay: Naushad, show me the first page at least as you are working on the second one now. (He was on the verge of panicking).

Naushad: Wait, I must show Physics sir that however hard questions he sets, I will crack all of them.

Sanjay was not able to believe the words of his friend as on one side he was struggling to pass and on the other side, Naushad was in some sort of competition or challenge with the teacher to prove his intellectuality. The last 10 minutes were left and

Sanjay felt like yelling at his pal but he kept his patience as he believed that at least now Naushad would show him the answers. But he was wrong. He was daydreaming as the final bell rang at the stipulated time and the Physics teacher asked everyone to submit their answer sheets.

This was the first instance that brought a slight difference in their newly made friendship. Sanjay felt a little bad about the whole episode. It hit him more when he failed the exam and Naushad was the topper in the subject. Nevertheless, Sanjay took an oath that he would double up his hard work.

One fine day Naushad and a few other friends suddenly arrived at Sanjay's house. Sanjay's mother was a bit orthodox lady and differentiated people based on religion. So, when she saw that Naushad was part of the gang, she sent a separate glass of water for him. Being a staunch devoted Hindu, she would discard this glass once Sanjay's friends have departed. Naushad was a Muslim and Sanjay's mother had her own traditional beliefs and faith. Well, Sanjay's friends and Naushad did not notice this, but he felt very awkward about the behavior of his mother.

This occurrence made him rethink the discriminating social fabric existing in our society and how this kind of approach is breaking our divine humanity. He promised himself that he will never teach or behave with the future generation with such a narrow-minded approach.

Naushad was a hunk and was quite popular among girls. Apart from his attractive looks, he was also a great athlete and performer. Being a district-level cricket player, he was already very popular in the school, and during any inter-school match, he would always don the jersey of the captain. As Sanjay too liked playing, Naushad always included him in the team. So, there was one girl named Shinaaya whom Naushad would often tease. He would do all kinds of mischievous acts to irate the girl, like would smile uncontrollably whenever she passed by him or would pass a silly amusing comment to grab her attention. In fact, on Valentine's Day, he sent 10 roses from 10 different people to her, and though she hated him for this, somewhere deep down she liked Naushad. She accepted all roses and refused none.

Once while the Math teacher was taking the class, one by one all the students started leaving the class and left to either the playground or the garden area for chit-chat. Naushad and Sanjay were the first ones to do the same. The reason was simple, his teaching style was not at all good, and none of the students used to comprehend what he wanted to explain. This continued for many days but one fine day he became very angry and asked the entire class to accompany him to the 'Principal' room. He complained to the head that the students always walk away from his class without even having the courtesy of informing him. The principal sir was quite a chilled-out person and he exclaimed in a very laid-back manner. "Sir as the Diwali festival is approaching, so let us all be lenient towards these students this time but yes if they do not change their approach, next time for sure we will take some action. So, excuse me now for the time being as I have some important work to do." All the students had a smile on their faces, though they pledged that they would not repeat this kind of wrong activity thereafter.

Everything changed with time. Very soon the entire batch reached 12th Standard. The fun-loving students had become serious as the board exam results would decide their future. Naushad and Sanjay too had started preparing for the same but they made sure that never miss their fun time.

One day when Naushad had gone out to the washroom, Anubhav came to Sanjay. (Anubhav, the same classmate who had met Sanjay on the first day of school).

Anubhav: Sanjay, I want to play a prank on Naushad. Let us put a nail on the place where he sits and this will tear his pant. It will be too much fun watching this.

Sanjay: This might hurt him Anubhav, so let us not do this.

Anubhav: Ok, I have an idea, the moment he starts sitting down, we will raise an alarm. This way we will not harm him and would have our share of fun also.

Sanjay: This sounds ok.

Sanjay went and kept the nail where Naushad used to sit. The moment Naushad arrived near his bench, from a very close distance he saw the nail embedded in the seat. He lost his cool and believing that Anubhav might have done this, he spoke out in an angry tone (Naushad never shared a good rapport with this guy and thus the first suspicion went on him).

Naushad: Whoever has done this, all my slang which I would utter now goes to him.

Sanjay: Naushad wait, I want to tell you something.

Naushad was in a fit of rage and did not want to hear anything. He went on blabbering ill words which somehow hurt Sanjay. He took every filthy jargon of Naushad on himself (which was not required at all). The jargons used were somewhere not digestible to Sanjay.

On top of that, Anubhav was trying to create a further rift in their relationship by igniting the already twisted situation. He tried convincing Sanjay that Naushad is doing all these things knowingly and he should take some action against him.

Anubhav: Sanjay, it seems your friend has got mad. How could he tell such words which are directly pitted against you?

Sanjay: Naushad has never been so angry. I do not know what has happened to him.

Anubhav: God bless him but your reaction seems very cool. If I were to be in your place, I would have hit him left and right.

And saying this, he left the spot with a sarcastic smile. Sanjay was hurt, even though all his friends tried to explain to him that all those abusive words which he spoke were for Anubhav and not for him. The entire class knew the enmity and jealousy that existed between both Naushad and Anubhav. But now Sanjay too was in no mood to hear anything and he stopped talking to Naushad. Both the friends stopped crossing each other's paths. If Sanjay saw that Naushad is walking toward him, he would make a U-turn and take a different direction. There was something that was going on in Sanjay's mind.

One afternoon when the students went out to play Volleyball, Sanjay intentionally stayed back in the classroom. After an hour he could see Naushad entering the class with a few of his friends. He straightway walked towards Naushad and punched him hard on his nose. Blood started oozing out and he fell to the ground. The entire class was stunned and there was a big uproar as nobody could understand what happened in a fraction of a second. Teachers ran in and caught Sanjay. He was immediately taken to the principal's office. The head of the school asked Sanjay to call his parents the next day. On the other side, Naushad was given first aid immediately and then sent to a nearby hospital.

Scared to death, Sanjay somehow narrated the entire episode to his father. His dad got very upset with him but then visited the school the day after. The principal was visibly distraught with the entire episode that transpired between the two friends. The moment Sanjay's father entered the office, he could easily gauge the same on the principal's disappointed face.

Father: Good morning, sir.

Principal: There is nothing good this morning. Your son is behaving like a terrorist. See how hard he had hit his companion (saying this he showed one of the pictures of Naushad with a bleeding nose). How can he be so violent and is this a common behavior prevalent in him?

Father: No sir, Sanjay is a very sincere child, I do not know the series of incidents that led to this but I firmly believe there might be a strong reason behind such a strong reaction from my son.

Principal: So, are you still justifying the act of your son? You know Naushad's parents could have made an FIR as this is a very serious case. Somehow, I managed to convince them to not do such a thing. This could have brought such a bad name to the school and would have spoilt the career of your child. Hope you are understanding the gravity of the situation.

Father: Absolutely sir and I am ashamed of the deeds of my son but would request you to excuse my son this time. I assure you that he will not repeat this erroneous act.

Principal: I am very sorry but I will have to suspend him for a week. I am saving your child from rustication as that is what Naushad's parents have asked for. But I will make them understand as this may ruin the future of your son but I cannot save him from suspension. One more thing, you will have to also sign a guarantee letter that your son won't recur this kind of activity again.

Father: (With a sad look) Ok sir and thanks for your consideration. I will sign the papers.

Sanjay's father knew that it is useless to scold him now as whatever must happen had happened. He was disheartened but he kept his emotions under control. The gloomy look on the face of his father broke Sanjay's heart and he knew something bad has happened.

The world of both Naushad & Sanjay broke down and it did not remain the same for both thereafter. They were subjected to frequent taunts from their teachers and peers. But they carried on as somewhere both had decided that they would prove to the world their worth fullness through their academic result. The two friends secluded themselves from social life and spent their entire time studying the curriculum for the 12th board exam. They got so captivated by their studies that sometimes their parents would forcibly ask them to take it a bit easy.

Soon the exams arrived and the entire batch appeared for the same. It went on for almost a month with a frequent interval after every test of a particular subject. Everybody gave their best. But this was not the end of it. Post the exams, most of the students were preparing for the entrance assessment for engineering and so were Sanjay & Naushad. After 2 months the results of the board exam came out and to everybody's surprise, Sanjay was the second topper of the batch and Naushad the 3rd ranker.

Though both friends were among the Top 10 students who were expected to deliver, nobody thought them to be in the Top 3. Their parents were enthralled to hear the news and after a long gap, the two friends were relieved.

Just two days later, Sanjay's father had thrown a party as he wanted to share his happiness with family and friends. He invited Naushad's parents as he believed in reconciliation. Through his life experiences, he knew that nothing is permanent and so any rivalry must have an ending.

In the evening, Naushad's parents were getting readied for the event wherein he was completely unaware of the same. Out of curiosity, he just asked his father.

Naushad: Hey, Dad. Where are you two planning to go and aren't I part of it?

Father: Who said that you are not accompanying us? Of course, you are part of it. So, get ready my boy, you would love the place where we are going.

For a second, Naushad got confused as he could not understand what his father meant by it but then dressed and joined the convoy. His father took the driving seat and accelerated the vehicle like a carefree youngster. Naushad could identify the route and he could see that it was leading to a place of which he is very aware. On the final turn, he exclaimed hurriedly.

Naushad: Dad, where are we heading towards? I think you are mistaken as this final turn will take us to Sanjay's house.

Father: Yes, we are going to his house only Naushad.

Naushad got furious and with a change in tone replied abruptly.

Naushad: I do not want to go, Dad. Please stop.

His father was in no mood to hear and parked his car near Sanjay's house. He dragged Naushad out of the vehicle. It was like how one treats a stubborn child. Sanjay's father was eagerly waiting for them as if they were the chief guest. In the center of the hall, there laid a big cake with a clear inscription on the top mentioned as "Congratulations Naushad & Sanjay". The hall was filled with all the friends of the duo and they all started screaming with excitement on seeing Naushad entering the house. Sanjay too was part of the group and he excitedly caught Naushad by his arm. He hugged him tightly as if the world is going to end today.

Sanjay: Congratulations my friend for being the 3rd topper of the school.

Naushad: Congrats to you also 2nd topper.

Sanjay: Let bygone be bygone. I am happy for you and pray to God that you get loads of success in the future.

Both friends cut the cake with joy in their eyes and hearts. The entire batch danced, sang songs, laughed, and played funny games at the party. Wow, what a night it was! A day that would remain evergreen in the hearts of all the people who were part of this occasion. Happy ending!!!!

Alone

Rahul was a reclusive child who would find it difficult to make friends. His mother was an Indian classical dancer who needed to travel to different locations for performances. Sometimes the duration would exceed more than a month. During that period Rahul would miss his mom a lot. The absence of any sibling in his life added to the misery. The only solace was the company of his father. During his career, his dad worked as a content writer in one of the reputed companies. But later, he left his flourishing job due to his son. He did not want Rahul to feel the absence of his mommy. It was the need of the hour as sometimes he would be found talking to himself. His mental strength had deteriorated. This worried his father a lot, he decided that he would now work as a freelance writer and work from home only. He wanted to devote some quality time to his son.

Slowly and gradually, Rahul developed an inseparable bond with his father. He was more of a friend than a guardian. For Rahul, his dad was the only friend he could rely on. He shared every minute detail of his life with him. He had his first cigarette with him and consumed alcohol for the first time in his company. His dad was the first person to know about his foremost crush. On multiple occasions, he had to respond to the calls of his son's teacher who complained of his mischievous deeds. It was ok as he had taught his son to not hurt or disrespect the feelings of others. Rest naughtiness is acceptable till the time it does not bring any financial or emotional loss to any.

There was nothing hidden between them. His dad had not kept any barrier knowingly. He knew Rahul very well. There were chances that if he did not hold his hand, he might fall into the company of bad people. To overcome loneliness, he could have taken the help of bad habits and people.

Rahul had always seen his dad as strong, both emotionally and physically. He had never seen tears in his father's eyes. Every morning he would see him going for a morning walk. Post, that regularly he would allot time for yoga. He did not have high Blood pressure and sugar which is prevalent among people of his age. Overall, his father was living a very healthy life.

Rahul wanted to become a commercial pilot but his mother was totally against it. The primary reason was the commercial aspect. The course required a lot of money, and they could not afford it even if they break their fixed deposits or a few savings in the bank and mutual fund. They did not have any properties which could have helped ease the situation. But at this crucial junction of his life, Rahul's dad firmly stood with him. He sold off his valuable assets to manage the commercials. Among them was his favorite car which he loved more than his life. Even after 5 years of existence, it looked brand new. Rahul's dad would clean and maintain it like a baby. Rahul was witness to the agony that his dad went through when he sold it off to the car dealer. He always kept smiling in front of him to hide his agony. But deep down inside, Rahul knew how painful it would have been for his father.

After two years of the course, with substantial flying experience, Rahul bagged his first job as a pilot in a renowned organization. The yearly remuneration was good and with his first salary, he bought gifts for his parents. After 3 years of job, he purchased an expensive car for his dad. This made his father quite emotional and he thanked his stars for having such an empathetic son.

Then came a time when Rahul fell in love with a girl and wanted to marry her. The challenge was that the lady belonged to a different religion. Her parents were totally against this marriage. Rahul knew that the only savior at this point could be his dad. Thus, he shared the issue with his father who swung into action immediately. He went to the girl's parent house to discuss the same. He explained to them, 'See now the children are asking our permission for the marriage because they both want us to be part of the ritual. They are trying to get all of us to agree on the nuptial. What if they just marry legally and don't even inform or invite us to the occasion? You will not be able to do anything. The law of the land would stand by their side. Society would rather taunt us saying that our kids did not even bother to inform their parents about their wedding. This would be quite a shameful and embarrassing thing for us. All we want is their happiness. If forcibly or by any other means we try to halt this marriage, then our kids would never remain content in their lifetime. So, please give them blessings and allow them to go ahead with the big decision of their life.'

Finally, the girl's family agreed but they had one condition. The marriage would happen according to their rites and rituals. Rahul's mother was against it but somehow his dad managed to convince her. The wedding happened with much fanfare.

Within a year of the marriage, Rahul's mother passed away. This was a big setback for him but his dad stood rock solid behind him. Though his father was distressed to lose his life partner, he held his emotions tight. He cried a lot but never in front of Rahul. He knew that if he loses mental strength now, Rahul would get shattered.

Time passed by, and slowly and gradually the family tried their best to overcome the grief. In life, on a day you face dark clouds, and then the next day is a burst of bright sunshine. Nothing is permanent, neither happiness nor sorrow. Very soon a piece of good news arrived in their life. Rahul's wife was three months pregnant. This made the atmosphere of the house very cheerful and jolly. Rahul's dad was very excited as after a long time something very good was going to happen in their otherwise depressed lives.

Things were looking quite upright in Rahul's life but then one day everything turned upside down. It was mid of August. The stormy weather outside was symbolizing some kind of disturbance around. Since very early morning, it was raining heavily that day. Around 8 am Rahul went to check on his dad for a cup of tea. Generally, after half an hour of yoga, he used to have a beverage. He could not find him in the room. The bathroom was open which meant that he was not inside. This made him a bit curious and he started checking every corner of the house, balcony, and bedroom but there was no trace of him. He started calling a few of his friends to check on him but failed miserably in locating him. This rose suspicion in his heart. Once again, he went back to his father's room to check if he has missed something. The doubts were true. On the study table, he found a letter folded very neatly. He immediately opened it to check on the content.

"I have left home to accomplish a few of the goals that I had planned to achieve in my life. Due to responsibilities, I could not follow my passion. Now it's the right time as you are well settled in your life. I need to get some time for myself.

Don't try to find me as I have left on my own. Contacting the police or anyone else is not at all required. Do not worry, nobody has kidnapped me. I am leaving for some unknown location. Once my goal is attained, I will connect with you. My phone number will remain switched off as I have taken an alternate number.

I would come back to see my grandson/granddaughter very soon.

God bless you!!!!!!

Your Loving Dad

Rahul took a deep sigh. It was as if his soul has left his body. There was a sense of vacuum left in his life. He just could not believe what he read just now. Nevertheless, he was in deep pain but at this point, he wanted to just move into a no-man zone land. His mentor, friend, and guide have betrayed him.

There was some sort of anger in his heart. How could his dad even think that he is well settled without him? His life without his dad was of no use.

With time every wound gets healed. But yes, the mark remains forever. There was not a single day when he would not remember his dad. Alas, the truth of his missing father pinched him every day.

A few months later Rahul was blessed with a baby boy. He missed his father's presence as he knew how much he wished to see the baby. But he had somehow accepted the decision his father had taken. Nevertheless, the bitterness against his father had grown more with time. He remembered on multiple occasions his dad would say that he wished to spend some time at a peaceful hill station. Therefore, there was no point in looking out for him. Rahul strongly believed that his father would one day surely come back to see his grandson. Now, whether that would be acceptable to him or not was a big question.

After a year and a half from the time Rahul's dad left the home, one day an unknown man, aged around 40-42 years walked up to his house. He was looking for Rahul as he has something important to convey. The unknown person introduced himself as Ajay. He conveyed that he had come from Nainital, a beautiful hill station. The unfamiliar man looked very peaceful and composed. He wore an ethnic dress and behaved like a courteous person. After glancing at the stranger for a while, Rahul finally broke the silence.

Rahul: ok, but what made you come here?

(Rahul was a bit curious and surprised as humility & humbleness showered from the visitor's approach. He did not look like the normal person that you see every day in your life).

Ajay: I have some bad news for you Rahul (His tone had turned sober).

This made Rahul a bit anxious. After all, what worse could happen in his life? He has lost his mother and he know nothing about the whereabouts of his father. The two most important people have already left him. Still, he was inquisitive to know about the fresh thunderstorm approaching his life.

Rahul: What is it? I am losing my patience. Kindly share the update.

Ajay: This piece of information is related to your dad.

The moment he heard this; his face turned red with anger.

Rahul: I do not want to hear anything about him. He left me when I needed him the most. What is the use of such a person in life who parts at a crucial junction of your life?

Ajay: What are you saying, Rahul? Are you serious or a nerd? Your dad spent all his life walking beside you so that you remain comfortable. He spent his fortune on building your career. He kept all his problems to himself and hid them from you so that you take a sound sleep. He never left you alone. He treated you like a friend and actively took interest in all your silly activities. Every responsibility that a good father should disburse, was done by him with complete accountability. He never disclosed to you that he is in the 3rd stage of cancer.

Rahul: What did you say? He is suffering from which disease?

Rahul got hysterical on hearing this.

Ajay: You heard it very right. He was diagnosed with cancer long back but he did not reveal this to you. Your dad left the home because he did not want his agonies to affect you. Never in his life was he ready to show his feeble and depleting body to you. Thus, he contacted us and we readily sheltered him. We own an Ayurvedic center in Nainital and take such acute cases.

Ajay once again started saying, 'Your father is in the final phase of blood cancer. The doctors have said that he can die at any moment. Your dad's last wish is to see his grandson. That is why I the caretaker of that center have come to inform this news personally to you.'

Rahul was filled with regrets. He understood that Ajay knew everything about their lives. He started reminiscing all those weak moments when his father stood right behind him to safeguard him. How could he say such a rude thing about his dad to a stranger?

Rahul immediately packed his bags and sat behind the wheels. Ajay and Rahul's wife along with their baby accompanied him in the vehicle. He drove at a lightning speed.

The moment they reached the shelter, Rahul docked the car and ran towards the entrance of the building. Ajay too followed him. He took Rahul to the room where his father was lying on the bed in a depleted condition. His eyes were closed and were in deep sleep. Rahul did not have patience and he woke his father.

Rahul: Dad, how are you? open your eyes. See, I have brought your grandson. You need to get up once for me.

Rahul was begging his father. He realized that his dad has very little time left with him. After continuous pleas by Rahul, his father finally opened his eyes after a lot of struggles. His dad could not utter a single word. But a smile flashed the moment he saw his grandson. He did not have enough strength to speak to them but he continuously kept his eyes open which showed a sign of hope and happiness.

Rahul sat beside his dad holding his hands the entire night. At around 4 am he woke to find his father's body had turned cold. His dad's eyes were closed by now but the sweet smile persisted on his face. Rahul did not panic as he understood that his father was gone. The smile on his face was proof that he had a peaceful exit.

He was devastated as the feeling of not being a good son shall prevail in his mind forever. There were hell lot of questions that would keep haunting him for the rest of his life. Why did he not search for his father for the entire year? Why did he think badly about him? Why did he speak harshly about his beloved dad? Why he did not appreciate the support that his dad provided?

There were so many 'why' which did not have an answer. He could only regret it as he could not stay and take care of his loving dad in his last days. The sense of guilt and shame would remain in his heart for a lifetime. He has lost his only friend forever.

You never know when the person you love is gone. So, always remain in touch and be kind to them. Especially your parents who burn their lives to light yours.

!!

Smile

Anamika was the eldest daughter of her parents and truly a responsible child. She behaved like an accountable guardian to her two younger siblings. Calm, composed, dignified, and answerable is something that she has imbibed in her nature. Her father was in a very reputable Central government job, part of the Human Resources department at a very senior designation. By the virtue of his post, he received all types of benefits from the organization, for example, a big residential house, a personal vehicle along with a driver, medical benefits, and so on. These materialistic things never impacted Anamika's behavior as she was grounded, easy to please, and a pleasure to be associated with. Her primary hobby was singing. She used to participate in different kinds of melody competitions organized in her locality, town, and school. Studying in Standard IX, in the best school in the region made her even more polished and dynamic. All in all, she was quite popular in her school due to her extra-curricular activities and elegant behavior.

Vedansh, the second protagonist of this story, on the other hand, was the youngest son in the family. Contrary to the notion that younger ones are pampered, he was quite disciplined and focused in life. Growing up with two elderly graceful sisters, he knew the boundaries to be drawn with friends, relatives, and strangers. He was too shy speaking to any girl and would turn red if directly confronted face to face with his lassie classmates. He was very specific about his association with friends and had only two or three pals with whom he was comfortable.

Both Anamika and Vedansh were in the same class in school but in different sections. Till standard 9th, both never got a chance to interact. But destiny had its plans. It so happened that both started taking physics and mathematics tuition from the same teacher. This allowed them to know each other. After school hours, they used to take their lunch in the class itself, and post that they used to walk down to the home of their teacher, thus getting enough time to comprehend each other.

The initial communication on their first day of tuition was torturous for Vedansh as he tried his best to avoid Anamika. On the other hand, Anamika was a bold girl who made the first move to break the ice.

Anamika: Hi, Vedansh. How are you?

Vedansh: (shyly) Hmm. Great. How do you know my name?

Anamika: I asked Anita and she gave me a detailed introduction about you (Anita was a common pal whose parents were close friends of the Vedansh and Anamika families). You have two elder sisters; your dad is a mechanical engineer and she went on ranting all minute information about him that she had gathered.

Vedansh: Wow. You are a quick learner. Aim for a profession in the Central Bureau of Investigation. Also, I am surprised as to why Anita gave you a such stretched introduction about me.

This is all that Vedansh could murmur in a low tone. More than that neither he was interested nor was he daring enough to carry on the communication any further. It was such a mean remark uttered by him, luckily she was not able to hear it.

There was one more character named Rohit in this story, who too was from the same school. His mother was a lecturer in one of the renowned institutes in the same town. She was very strict and was known for her integrity in the university. Somehow Rohit's personality got subdued due to the scrutiny and strict supervision of his mom. Both Vedansh and Rohit were good friends. They preferred solitary living. The nice part was that together they found solace in each other's company.

Anita and Rohit too joined the same tuition class. Anamika was the chirpiest among them and always had some pre-defined plans for the group. One day she requested her dad to send the company vehicle to pick them up from tuition and drop them at their respective homes. Vedansh, Rohit, and Anita were quite a bit surprised as they were not used to such kinds of luxuries but who could say no to such comforts? On the way, Anamika bought candies and chocolates for all of them, and the entire group played dumb charade games the entire journey.

Her smile and sweet nature were infectious, and it had started showing magic on everyone especially Vedansh. He started to open slowly and gradually.

Vedansh: Thank you Anamika. I wish we should have been friends earlier.

Anamika: And, why is that so?

Vedansh: I would have got this delicious chocolate from you long back then.

Anamika: So, mean of you Vedansh.

And both laughed heartily. Slowly Vedansh had become active in the group. Now the challenge was to make this cluster more vibrant. Rohit and Anita were still not that close to Anamika. But Anamika was on a mission to create a strong bond among the four friends. To make this successful, the next day she informed the rest three pals that her father is once again sending the vehicle one more time, so they should make the most of it. Nobody responded to her call except Vedansh.

Vedansh: Sure Anamika. What do you all say, guys?

Vedansh shoved Rohit a bit to reply.

Rohit: Sure. I am in.

Vedansh: Great. Anita, now you too must show some enthusiasm.

Anita: OK. I am in, too. (She had no option but to join)

The next day after tuitions, on the way back home they dropped by for an hour at a very beautiful guest house that had an awesome garden with greenery spread across the plot. The four of them spent an enjoyable one-hour span of time joking and pulling each other legs at the scenic location.

Rohit: I think we should have come here earlier. We have seen this guest house every day on our daily route to school trip but never got a chance to visit it. Thanks to our Goddess Anamika who made it possible.

Vedansh: Agree with you Rohit 100%. We are nothing without her.

Anita: What about me guys? Do you regret meeting me?

Vedansh: Yes (with a very serious note)

Everybody started laughing. Anita hit Vedansh with an irritated look.

Among all these friends Vedansh and Anamika shared a very different bond, at least this is what Vedansh believed. But things were going to change very soon.

After one complete year which was full of hard work and labor, all four finally passed the 9th Standard and entered the very crucial year of their lives, the 10th board. Tuitions classes continued but their mode of travel had changed now. Every day all four friends used to commute by private bus. In this one-hour journey, they all would not leave a single instant of teasing each other. Vedansh made a point that he sits beside Anamika in the vehicle. He liked spending time with her. Whenever she was around, there remained positivity and happiness in his life.

Mohan, another common friend of all four has a crucial role in the story. He liked Anamika and had expressed his feelings to her. The challenge was that after school hours, he hardly got any time to be with her. So, he made a point that on weekends when both school and tuitions were off, he would come to visit Vedansh at his house. And then together they would go to Anamika's house.

Once Anamika invited all their friends to her house on her birthday. She had called all her three friends and Mohan for the celebration. As usual, they started pulling each other's legs.

Vedansh: Anamika, where is the cake? See Mohan has come all the way to get a piece of the dessert.

Anamika: Mohan, is it true?

Mohan: Oh! No. Vedansh can you stop, please?

Rohit: I am in complete agreement with Vedansh. Mohan had just come for the cake. Otherwise, what could be his other motivation?

Anita: I too agree with Vedansh and Rohit.

Mohan: You all always gang up against me. It seems I am the scapegoat of this group.

The way Mohan cribbed about the same, brought a smile to the face of everyone. They sang, danced, and enjoyed for another couple of hours and then left for their respective homes after a pleasant evening.

Vedansh had a liking for a girl who studied in the same section where Anamika belonged to. One day he shared his feelings for the girl with Anamika with a strict note to not discuss the same with anyone. On divergent, she gulped down everything in front of the same girl for whom Vedansh had a soft corner.

He was not aware of the same until the next day during the lunch break when he found Anamika and the girl whose name he had mentioned to Anamika, heading toward him. This instantly gave him an impulse that something is wrong. He ran in the opposite direction as he did not want to face them. After some time, he turned to check whether they are following him or not. Convinced that they have left, he moved towards his classroom. But to his astonishment, both Anamika and the girl were patiently waiting for him at the entrance of the class. There was no way he could have escaped. He still tried but was caught red-handed. They started grilling him with questionnaires that made him quite uncomfortable. To avoid any controversy, he tried ignoring their queries. His action could not prevent them from interrogating him. They started probing him;

Girl: Vedansh, tell me why have you mentioned my name to Anamika? What are your intentions behind this?

Instead of helping him, Anamika was standing with the girl as if she is her guardian. To make the matter worse, she too started questioning him in support of the girl.

Anamika: Tell us Vedansh, what is the reason behind it?

Vedansh: Excuse me, girls, see the lunch is already over. The teacher may show up at any time, so please leave me now. For sure I would tell the truth in the next one to two days. Saying this he rushed into the room.

For the next 2-3 days, he maintained a completely low profile and did not venture beyond his classroom. He remained tight seated in the class, even during the morning prayer. Luckily the storm passed by and things became normal as the girls never came back to cross-examine him. For a few days, he even stopped talking to Anamika.

Very soon 10th board exams arrived and all the students began preparing for the same. Just 2 months before the exams, a farewell party was organized for the departing class. This was conducted by the immediate junior i.e. 9th standard pupils, and supported by the school management. The entire batch wore Indian attire, girls in sarees, and boys in kurta pajamas. Anamika was looking gorgeous and so were the other girls. Vedansh could not resist commenting on her.

Vedansh: Aunty, where do you live?

Anamika with a surprised look turned back and with an irritated tone reacted.

Anamika: Hello, none of your business uncle.

Vedansh: Copycat

With an ironic smile, he left the place.

There were lots of songs, dances, and entertainment programs the whole evening. Delicious food and drinks were served in the buffet. Blessings along with best wishes for the exams were given by teachers and the principal. The pupils were overjoyed and happy with the grand sendoff they had received. A pinch of sadness was also palpable in the hearts of the students as most of them would leave the school forever for greener pastures.

A vehicle had arrived for Anamika and thus all three friends hopped in the automobile. Vedansh was gloomy as he was going to miss his school and his lovely friends. The rest three, Rohit, Anamika, and Anita were trying to cheer him up by saying that they are friends forever and would keep in touch with each other, no matter wherever they are.

Soon the exams started and all the preparations that students have done for it was going to be tested now. One by one, the assessment papers got over, and soon the last day arrived for which the entire batch had waited patiently. They believed that post this they would get freedom from all stress and worries (that is what they assumed). Once the paper got over, everyone took a sigh of relief. It was as if they all have got a respite from some kind of unsolicited tension. Vedansh wanted to discuss something with Anamika and thus went to her class to check on her. She was not there, so he searched all the probable places where she usually used to hang out with her friends. He tried hard but she was nowhere to be seen. Thus, the very next day he went to meet her at her house but to his dismay, the door was locked. The neighbors said that the family has left for some other place as Anamika's father got a sudden transfer posting to some unknown location. He just could not believe it as he never expected such an odd ending to their friendship. As there is an old saying, 'Too much expectation leads to frustration" and that is what happened with Vedansh. He just could not believe yet that Anamika left the place without meeting him or informing him about her whereabouts.

Time flies and leaves behind all those lovely memories. Once when Vedansh had completed his 12th board exams, from somewhere he got the news that Anamika is studying in a particular city at a renowned college. As he was supposed to give one of the entrance exams in the same location, so he planned to drop by Anamika's hostel to check on her. He was too excited as he would be meeting Anamika after two long years. In the visitor's room of the hostel, the warden was sitting on her chair with a grumpy face.

Vedansh: Good morning mam. Can you please call Anamika? I have a message to deliver which her father has asked me to do so.

Warden: Are you sure you know her?

Vedansh: (stammering) Yes mam.

Warden: Then for that, you will have to visit her father's place as she left for the same just 2 days back.

Stunned and embarrassed by the warden's reply he hurriedly left the place. He was sad but things were not in his hand. There is no one bigger than destiny.

Time is the best healer and Vedansh throughout this period got busy with his studies. He did his graduation and then worked for two years abroad in a multi-national organization. Post that he returned to his homeland as he was the only son in the family and wanted to take care of his parents.

On social media, he was quite active, and so on one of the sites, he found Anamika as its member. Out of curiosity, he checked her profile but then with an unknown thought stopped further encroachment as he felt a sense of detachment. To his surprise, the very next day he got a message on the same social media site from her, "Hey, you checked my profile and left without leaving any message for me, very mean of you". He wanted to reply but there was something that again prompted him to step back and stay mute.

Days passed by, and still, the two friends did not get a chance to catch up with each other. But as you say destiny has its say and so once again out of nowhere, they crossed paths. Five years later, it so happened that Vedansh got transferred to the same city where Anamika was based. He was aware of the same but did not try connecting with her. She was married by then and had one kid. Vedansh too was in a committed relationship with two children from his wife. None of them tried to make the first move to contact, even though they were part of various social media groups of common friends. Somewhere Anamika knew that Vedansh is hurt as it was she who did not have the courtesy to inform him when she left the town many years back. Thus she took the initiative and called her friend as somewhere deep inside she wanted to make up for the time they had lost due to their busy lives.

Anamika: Hey Vedansh. How are you? Long time. We should meet someday Vedansh?

Vedansh: Why? (it seemed as if he was not at all keen on a meeting)

Anamika: (Surprised to hear the question) What do you mean by 'why'? Don't you want to see me ever again?

Vedansh: Yes, but a lot of time has passed by Anamika. I even do not remember now your likes and dislikes.

Anamika: Hello, I just want to meet you. Don't worry I am not going to propose to you for marriage. So, chill. Let us meet up.

Vedansh: Ha-ha, as if I was waiting for you to ask me for the same.

Anamika: Do not show your coolness here, mister. Tomorrow I am coming to see you at your office. I know it is on Park Street, so just message me the address (she instructed like a boss).

Vedansh: Ok mam, as you say.

He messaged the office details to her and waited patiently for the next day. Vedansh had a kind of mixed feelings as he was excited that they were meeting finally but was a bit sad as they should have been in touch earlier. On the other hand, Anamika was super thrilled as she was missing the company of her dear friend, she woke early in the morning and started completing her daily chore of household work hurriedly. Post finishing all her jobs, she got ready to meet her pal. She booked a taxi as she was already late for the day. Just 5 minutes before she was about to reach the location, she tried calling Vedansh. To her bewilderment, his phone was switched off. A bit confused and disheartened, she hung up her phone. She started thinking and praying that she meets Vedansh today anyhow.

It so happened that Vedansh's phone got switched off due to some technical issue and he was not able to turn it on. Unfortunately, he did not remember Anamika's number which prevented him from connecting and informing her about the same. Though Vedansh had shared the location and building number, he missed sharing the floor and room as to where he would be seated. Neither did he share the company name where he was working. The building had multiple offices on various floors and so when she reached there, she just had only one piece of information and that was the name of his friend. On entering the corporate office, she straightaway headed towards the reception.

Anamika: Excuse me, can you please tell me where is the office of Mr. Vedansh Kumar?

Receptionist: (Looking amused) Mam there are thousands of people working in multiple enterprises. How would

I know each one of them by name? If you can please identify the company in which your friend is working, then I would be able to guide you.

Anamika: In that case, why would I require your help? (She got irritated)

She was getting impatient and sad with every passing moment. She decided that she would hold on at the waiting lounge for some time, anticipating Vedansh might be trying to reach her. Anamika knew that there would be a genuine reason behind the unavailability of her friend. Except for a fading hope, she had nothing more to say or do. On the other hand, Vedansh took his phone to a mobile repair shop hastily where the shop owner informed him that the phone is dead and that it would take at least 48 hours to revive it. It was already 1:30 pm and they had planned the meet at around 1 pm. Vedansh had lost all hope of seeing Anamika this time and he could visualize history repeating. The only difference was that this time Anamika was waiting for Vedansh. The moment he entered the gallery of his office, somebody from the back gave a friendly push. Vedansh turned around to find Anamika giving a very vivacious smile. For a moment it seemed that the time had stopped and they both were in a no-time zone. Then on regaining the consciousness, they both hugged each other as if they have not met for ages.

Vedansh: Wow, so finally you are here.

Anamika: I was destined to meet you one day and see I am here.

Vedansh: Let us go to the coffee shop as I have lots and lots of things to discuss.

Both behaved like teenagers, laughing off at every casual joke. They kept on chit-chatting for a long time. For those few hours, they were able to recreate the bond that had been lost for years due to all those unavoidable circumstances. Finally, Vedansh had to leave as it was office hours and he could not stay there for long. Promising each other that they would remain in contact henceforth, left for their respective destination.

Vedansh's smile was back as he knew that it was Anamika who had taught him to keep smiling even when you find nothing worthwhile in life. Happiness is when you see your best friend's smiling face, isn't it?

Unspoken

The last two weeks were quite tough for Ryan. Five years of marriage with his wife had ended abruptly. Finally, the two got divorced legally. There was a clear sign of depression on his face and he seemed lost. He would keep on thinking about all those moments spent in the fight, love, and hatred between him and his spouse. Good or bad, he recalled all those memories. Sometimes, he would cry his heart out. This would temporarily relieve his broken heart. Occasionally, he would keep on staring blankly at the ceiling. The house which was always well maintained and decorated, now was in a complete mess. A layer of dust and dirt had covered the entire carpet area. Personal hygiene too was missing as an untrimmed beard and uncut hair revealed the shabby truth. He would miss taking bath, the frequency would be after every three or four days. It was as if Ryan had lost interest in everything. He owned a pharmacy shop that he did not visit for a week (He possessed a pharmacist degree). It remained close as he did not wish to go to work. He stayed back at home, lazily sleeping on the bed or sluggishly lying on the couch located in any corner of the house. Ryan would either order some kind of fast food from the app or would survive on ready-to-eat stuff. He majorly sustained on beverages and would munch a proper diet just once in the whole day.

Ryan had stopped attending any calls irrespective of the cruciality of the same. He wanted to isolate himself from his kith and kin. Anyways this did not matter to him as in the name of family, he only had a sister who was 700 miles away from the place where he lived in. She hardly visited or interacted with him. Both his mom and dad had passed away long back. In terms of friends, he was not in good standing with any. Thus, at a time when he needed a kind of support system, there was no one around him. It was the ultimate pitiful state that one could ever imagine. All in all, he was living a dry life devoid of any emotional backing that could have helped him in healing the sad state of mind that he was going through.

There was just one good habit that he was following despite all those setbacks in his life. He never missed the early morning jogging. Ryan was consistent and followed this routine religiously. He hated encountering known people on the way. In that way, he was lucky as the count of early risers was anyways low. Being an introvert, he naturally enjoyed such an isolated atmosphere. He could foresee some kind of positivity while facing the sun rising and slowly enlightening the whole sky.

On one such walk; he came across an approximately 1-year-old Labrador puppy looking misplaced and tired. It had a beautiful golden collar around its neck, meaning somebody owned it. He looked around to see if the owner is nearby. He could find none which meant the pet has lost its way or someone had just discarded it. Ryan never loved or had an affinity for pets. Thus, he just ignored it at the very first instance and walked away. But then the little puppy started following him. The more he tried to get away from it, the more the little dog kept shadowing Ryan. At one point it started licking his legs. This act just melted his heart. The canine was in an inebriated state, ragged, worn out, and hungry. He took hold of the small creature and brought it to his home. The first thing that he did was clean and give the puppy a nice bath. The cute baby dog was hungry, thus he fed it with milk. Then he googled out various food items that can be given as a portion of the diet for the Labrador. A small pet shop was nearby that kept various kinds of food and nutrition for the homely animals. He prepared a small bed out of the pillow for the puppy. This was not an act of kindness, instead, Ryan had started loving the dog. For him, it had become part of his life now. Every day in the morning he would take it out for a walk. They would spend hours strolling on the beach. Both would have breakfast, lunch, and dinner together. The innocent little dog would also watch TV with its master. They would together play various puppy games together. Lovingly he started calling the dog by the name 'Dazzy.'

It was high time for Ryan, as the chemist's shop had remained closed for more than a month. In this span, he had spent a fortune on himself and his dog. Now, he was running short of finances. He had to get back to work. Finally, he went to open his shop. The only challenge was that he must keep Dazzy back at the home. He followed this for the next two days but this started giving panic attacks to him. He was deeply concerned about the well-being of the puppy. The canine was also getting depressed seeing its owner leaving it all alone every day. In the evening when he used to come back, the dog would not come close to him in anger. Thus, to stop all this, he started taking Dazzy along with him to the outlet. He would tie the canine just outside the shop. It was a very friendly dog who adored children. The kids would flock to his shop to just play with the puppy. Time flies, 6 months passed by and now the puppy had grown into a full-grown adult.

Ryan planned a trip to a nearby hill station which was around 200 km from the town. He packed everything in his car and then took 'Dazzy' along with him. He was looking for some kind of peace and fun, far away from the hustle and bustle lifestyle back in the city. The dog had become his only friend. It was as if it understood every feeling of the human who was its caretaker. The moment it found that Ryan was sad, it would jump in his lap to comfort him. It was a short two-day trip and both were spontaneously strengthening their bonds together. While in the hills, Ryan planned solo trekking along with Dazzy. The staff of the hotel where he stayed warned them not to do so as wild animals were roaming around freely in the rock surrounded by beautiful flora & fauna. Ryan did not pay heed to the suggestion and started the expedition the very next day in the early morning. It was a 20 km trip to and from the hotel. The duo would have hardly crossed 2 Km when out of nowhere a wild fox got spotted. It looked very angry and started growling on seeing the pair. This brought the Labrador into action. It started barking ferociously as if it was saying 'Better be away from my master, don't even dare to put any footstep towards him.' But the fox was in no mood to listen, it ran aggressively toward Ryan. Dazzy jumped into the middle to face the wild animal. The two canines scratched and wrestled with each other in their bid to establish dominance. The fox tried to lunge at the Dazzy's neck but was unsuccessful. On the other hand, Dazzy bit the claws of the fox. This made it retreat in the bush. Once the battle was over, Ryan ran toward his pet to caress. He was too grateful to see his friend risking its life to safeguard him. Dazzy was injured as there was a deep cut mark on the neck. The canine almost collapsed in his lap. He carried it back to his hotel to provide first aid. Being a pharmacist, he knew what needs to be given in this scenario. He drove back to the town the same afternoon as he wanted to take no risk. It was urgent to show Dazzy to a veterinary doctor. Luckily there was no tissue damage and thus did not require any kind of surgery. The medic put a certain lotion on the wound to help kill the germs and then applied an antibiotic for preventing any further infection. In a week, Dazzy was up and healthy.

The company of Dazzy helped Ryan in healing most of his agonies and pains. One day while Ryan was on his way to the pharmacy, he saw photos of a Labrador puppy on consecutive billboards placed at the sides of the footpath. The message below the picture was as below, 'Dear All, Unfortunately, we lost our 1-year-old Labrador pet 'Rambo' a few months back. A golden collar around the neck is the identity mark. If anybody finds it, kindly call me on mobile no. 97330*****'. He was shocked to see it. It was as if the ground has started slipping under his feet. Ryan took a snap so that he could verify the same later. In the evening while at home, he once again checked the picture that he has taken on the day when he brought Dazzy to his home. He zoomed in to validate, and to his dismay, the golden collar matched (it was like what he had located for the first time when he had found the puppy). He instantly decided that he would not call the owner as he could not think of his life without his new pet.

Two days passed by. There was something that was giving Ryan sleepless nights. All the time he would keep discerning of Dazzy. What would happen if the real owner takes away the canine from him? How would he live without it? Then parallelly thoughts of his ex-wife came haunting back. The pain of separation that he had to undergo had not completely vanished from his life. But then around all these feelings, one thing that stroked him was how would the family be feeling who had lost its dog. They too would be in a lot of suffering. He can feel the distress of losing someone very close to him ardently. This made him dial the number of the person who was broadly mentioned in the hoarding. The phone was picked up by a kid who before hearing anything just said that 'Mom and Dad are outside and the moment they come, they will call you back'. Saying this the child dropped the call. Just after an hour, he received a call back where a man named Adam introduced himself. 'Hi, I am Adam. Received your call while I was out for some work. My little girl told me you were looking for me. Do I know you by any chance? Ryan replied, 'Mr. Adam, I saw the advertisement that you had put about your lost dog 'Rambo'. I am afraid it is the same dog that I have been petting for over a few months.' Ryan then went on to explain how, when, and where he found the puppy. The circumstance and timing matched when the real owner had lost the canine.

The very next morning the family arrived at Ryan's place to check on the dog being taken care of by Ryan. Dazzy was playing with the toys provided by its owner. On seeing it, the tiny girl, aged around 7 immediately called out the name of the canine 'Rambo'. At first, the animal looked confused but then after some time the dog responded and ran toward the girl. It was overjoyed on seeing its real owners. It just swirled and circled the family for another fifteen minutes in excitement. The family was in hurry and they wanted to leave as soon as possible. Once they had thanked Ryan for his kind act, they tied a new leash around the dog's neck and started to move toward their parked vehicle. The canine was not moving at all and the family had to drag it into the car. They all were perplexed as to why the dog is behaving so indifferently. The kid ran back toward Ryan and once again profusely expressed gratitude for taking care of their pet. She asked for a photo of Ryan. Ryan was surprised, he exclaimed:

Ryan: Why do you need my snap?

Kid: Sir, in case 'Rambo,' misses you, I would show your picture to it.

Ryan: And how do you know that it is going to miss me?

Kid: I can comprehend sir. You took very good care of my dog. 'Rambo' seemed very happy with you. I can read its eyes. I also feel strongly that right now it is very sad. Leaving you would have been very difficult for it.

Ryan: Thank you, dear. You are an empathetic girl. I am going to badly miss my 'Dazzy' and your 'Rambo' (saying this he took a big sigh). My birthday is just a week later, so, if possible, please do a video call with our dear pet on that day. I would be highly obliged.

Kid: Certainly, I would do that.

The kid grabbed the photo of Ryan and ran back to the car where her parents were waiting impatiently for her to come.

There was complete silence in the heart and house of Ryan. Tears started rolling down his eyes the moment the family left the place. He felt as if someone very personal and precious has departed him forever. Unable to bear the pain, he opened a bottle of Scotch Whiskey. He knew that this is the only option to calm down his nerves. He drank till late at night. The next morning, he woke up with complete dizziness. He did not even remember at what time he slept. One thing that 'Dazzy' had taught him was that show must go on. You need to move on and keep doing your job. So, without wasting any time he left for the shop. The entire day he remained busy with the customer. He did not get a single moment to remember his beloved pet. But the moment he arrived at his home, there was ample stillness. He started recollecting what he used to do for the dog once he used to come back to the house. Playing with it, making its favorite food, and then listening to his favorite music. Hardly he would get any time left out for himself. But now alas he had nothing much to do. Slowly he dragged himself towards the bookshelf and picked a fiction novel from it.

A week passed by and it was his birthday. He was reminiscing old childhood days when a birthday would be an occasion to celebrate. Friends & family would wish and you would be the epic of attraction. At present, he has no one with whom he can spend time. He wished himself a very happy birthday and left for his outlet. This was just another day for him. In the evening, he bought a bottle of champagne from the liquor shop. He knew he would require this. The moment he reached his house, he found a drum size box wrapped in multicolored gift paper. It made him a bit curious. There was a beautifully tied ribbon on the top, which he tried to open. But before he could do it, he could hear the barking of the dog. He immediately realized that it was 'Dazzy.' He hurriedly unwrapped the box to bring out the canine. The pet looked so happy on seeing Ryan. Even Ryan was on top of the world. He was unable to share his happiness and emotions. From behind, a sweet voice singing 'Happy Birthday to You,' startled him. It was the same kid and her family wishing Ryan a very happy birthday. They had brought a beautiful cake with them for Ryan.

Ryan immediately invited them inside. Dazzy excitedly entered the room as if he has entered its original den. It kept on licking Ryan's face non-stop. Ryan just could not believe his luck. He was not able to understand what is happening around him. To clarify the air of confusion, he asked the kid;

Ryan: Kiddo, I had just asked you to do a video call so that I could see Dazzy. But I am thankful that you brought it here just for me.

Kid: We did not have any other option, sir.

Ryan: What do you mean by it?

Kid: Sir, the day when we brought it from you to our house, your 'Dazzy' and our 'Rambo' started behaving very differently. He had stopped eating. It even missed its favorite diet of roasted chicken. This had never happened before. You remember I had taken a snap of yours. It would keep looking at it for hours in our house. We realized that we have lost our 'Rambo.' It now prefers to be 'Dazzy'. The words were **'unspoken'** but we could easily understand what it wanted. That is why we thought of bringing it back to you forever.

Ryan: Are you sure or am I daydreaming? I just could not believe what I heard.

Kid: No, sir. This is the ultimate reality.

Ryan: Thanks a lot. This is the most prized gift I ever received on my birthday. God bless you.

Ryan served the family with champagne that he had on the way home. He ordered online food for them. Meanwhile, he cut the cake and everybody wished him again. After spending two hours at Ryan's house the family left. He lovingly picked up the canine to caress and pamper it. He felt as if God had given him a new lease on life. His faithful friend is back with him again. All is well that ends well.

Friends Forever

Today was the day two years back when Rita had lost her husband. She had lit candles in front of her hubby's picture and made the dishes he loved. It was a way of keeping his fond memories alive. The first six months after his demise was very painful. They had two kids who had grown into adults when she lost her hubby. Both children, a boy, and a girl were married and thus after two weeks of mourning their father's death, they all left for their respective locations (where they were well-settled). They kept on insisting Rita accompany them but she remained adamant. She was not ready to leave the house that she and her husband had erected with lots of love and affection. Her son became quite angry as he did not want to leave her all alone in the large vacant 4-bedroom house kitchen villa. Though he cared for her, he knew that his mother was a strong lady. Even at 63 years of age, she was filled with grit, confidence, and determination. Aside from that, she had been living in the neighborhood for 25 long years. It was a cooperative society that belonged to people who had worked in the same organization for 30-35 years together. Post-retirement, many of them shifted to this place and were living quite a peaceful life. Thus, quite a safe and secure place to live in.

Rita had a lot of friends in the locality. Every day they would gather at Rita's home for chit-chat. They also had a kitty group of 8 ladies who assembled at each other's house every month. They would have fun activities, drinks, and food at the gathering. This social group was a kind of savior for her. Any kind of problem, her friends would immediately stand by her. She found a sense of security and solace among her networks. The pain of losing her life partner was too much for her. It was this circle of pals who tried their best to heal the agony of losing their dearest companion. If she was not well, any one of them would take her to the doctor's place. If she needed some kind of product from the main market that was far off distant place, somebody would accompany her in a hired conveyance like an auto, taxi, etc. For small issues, she did not want to concern her children. They were almost 700-800 miles away, so did not wish to disturb them at the drop of a hat.

Rita would have all the news of people residing in the society. She never played politics because of which everyone liked to share their issues with her. She knew all the problems that her friends were facing in their respective lives. Out of 8 ladies of the kitty party group, two of them were very close to her, Divya and Ashwini. Divya like her was a widow whose husband has passed away 5 years back. She had two sons who did not treat her quite well. They did not live with her and would come to the place once a year only to discuss the division of property among themselves left by her hubby. Shamelessly they would have an open conversation with their mother without thinking about how hurt she would feel. The second friend Ashwini and her hubby had only one daughter who did not believe in the institution of marriage. She desired to remain unmarried lifelong. No matter what opinion her daughter had in her mind, Ashwini would keep trying her best to somehow push her girl to look for husband-material boys. She always remained in tension for her child as there was no one to take care of her once they as a parent had left this materialistic world. Rita felt pity for the conditions of his two dear friends but could not do anything about it.

One day, the president of the society announced that there would be an emergency meeting the day after. One member of each family needed to be present in the same. The society meetings were mostly attended by male members but, Rita had to be part of it due to the absence of any representative from her house. On the said day, the allocated room was filled and everyone wanted to know the context of the sudden assembling. The President took the center stage and with a smile started speaking, "My dear friends, as the head of the society it's my duty to provide the best of services to you and your family. Many residents have been recently complaining to me about the bitter taste and the toxic quality of water stored in the overhead tanks in each villa. So, I have planned a routine cleaning of the reservoir as per your request. Just houses H10 to H14 will have the same cleaned after some months due to the financial crunch in the resident fund. But I assure you that the same would be done before the Durga Puja which is just 4 months ahead". There was a thunderous clap from the audience as this essential work was the need of the hour. Children and adults were falling ill due to the contaminated water. The only unhappy people were the families residing in villas H10 to H14. And the count of it was just 2 as H11, H12 & H13 were vacant for the moment. Rita was very angry, her house H10 was excluded from the regular cleaning as announced by the president. She felt cheated and betrayed. "How can they single out just 2 houses? It was as if her priorities were sidelined due to the absence of any male member representing her family". This question was continuously popping at the top of her head at the moment. Unable to hold on to the thought, she suddenly screamed in the meeting. "This is injustice as you cannot single out just two of us". This sudden outburst startled everyone. But the President ignored it as if he has not gotten anything. He moved out of the room avoiding any direct interaction with Rita. This further infuriated her but for the first time in her life felt quite helpless. In the male-dominated representation where all the portfolio holders like the general secretary, treasurer, etc. were being held by them, it became impossible for her voice to be heard. But she was determined to make a stand and challenge the faulty authority. Alone she could have failed, thus she needed support.

In the evening, she called all her friends to her house and shared the sad ordeal. The ladies planned a protest against the president in the early morning. They prepared placards with slogans like "We want justice" and stood in front of his house. Rita was leading the pack. One of her friends had links in the media, and thus she had called a reporter to cover it. The President on seeing the mayhem outside his house became quite nervous but was not ready to bend. The friends stood there for 6 long hours but in vain. From there on, they went for the second strategy. The next day in a very popular newspaper an article came out about the biased approach of the President. This brought the local politicians into action and they spoke to President to immediately revoke his partial approach or face action. Scared, the very next day he announced that water tank cleaning will happen for the entire society including H10 and H14. Rita and her group of ladies were happy with the decision. They all celebrated the power of unity by having a small tea party in the evening.

One day Ashwini cheerfully came to Rita's house and exclaimed, 'Rita, my daughter has finally said 'yes' to the marriage. Rita wanted to understand who persuaded Ashwini's daughter to marry. But this was a piece of good news and it was not the right time to put such a query in front of her friend. Rita excitedly asked, 'Have you found any suitable boy for her'? Ashwini replied, 'Yes, one of my close relatives has suggested this person who works in a multinational bank as the branch manager. The family is good and there is no dearth of wealth & property among them. Even I have done the background check and found that they are good people.' Rita was glad to hear that but still had some doubts. She wanted to check whether her daughter's choice has been considered or not. Ashwini clarified that by saying that her kid was ok with the proposal and that is why she has come to Rita. This confused Rita as she wanted to comprehend what role she needed to play here.

Ashwini started removing the clouds of jumbled equations by saying, "Rita, before saying the final 'yes' to the groom's family, I want to meet the prospective groom at his office. We hear a lot of fraud cases now and then. I want to be double-sure before affirming this relationship. Thus, I need your help. I am not able to gather enough courage to check on him at his workplace. I feel nervous as you know I have not even completed my graduation. Also, I am not very acquainted with the professional culture of the current generation. I feel very shy but because of my daughter, I will have to overcome this. Please accompany me to the boy's official location.'

Rita was a bold lady. In her society, everybody knew that she had done Masters in Arts during the days when girl children were not allowed to study much. High school was the maximum, they could have achieved academically. But her father was quite forward-thinking and pushed her child to the route of learning. It's a different story that Rita could not convert her credentials for monetary benefit. Before her marriage, she was the assistant lecturer for Economics at a renowned institute in the city. After marriage, just 1 year later, her daughter got born. She had to choose between her career and family, and she opted for the latter, resigning from her coveted profession.

Coming back to the story, Rita agreed to go with her friend Ashwini to verify the genuineness of the groom. They left for the bank together and the moment they entered the office, they saw a help desk where a lady was seated. Rita straightaway headed towards the counter. On seeing Rita and Ashwini standing in front of her, the lady questioned:

Lady: How, may I help you, mam?

Rita: We wanted to meet the branch manager.

Lady: What is the issue mam? I can surely assist you if you do not mind.

Rita insisted on meeting the branch manager as there was something that she could only discuss with the person in charge. Seeing the adamant approach of both the ladies, she allowed them to meet the division head after taking due permission from him.

The head of the branch (the groom) was engrossed in some kind of work on his laptop. He very politely asked the ladies to have a seat.

> Branch Manager: Mam, why did you take the pain of coming to the office? You could have informed someone from the branch, they would have readily visited your place. At this age, you should just take care of your health.

Such soothing and beautiful words from the person melted their hearts. They could not pretend any further of being customers. Thus, Ashwini introduced herself, saying that she is the mother of the girl whom he is going to marry. She also familiarized him with Rita who was her best friend. The boy was overwhelmed to hear that. He touched the feet of both the ladies to take their blessings. Simultaneously, he ordered a cup of tea for both. After having the beverage and doing normal chit-chat with the future husband of her daughter, they both left the office. While leaving, Rita wanted to check the real personality of the branch manager once again. So, while she was out of the bank, she started conversing with the security guard of the division. Rita exclaimed, 'Your branch manager is very rude. He does not know how to behave with the customers.' The guard's reply mesmerized them and they were pleased to hear that. He said, 'Mam, there might be some kind of confusion. As far as I know, our branch manager is the kindest soul on earth. He goes out of his way to help a needy person. So, kindly do not use such harsh words for him in front of me.'

This was more than enough to confirm that Ashwini has selected the right person for her daughter. In the very next month, the marriage ceremony got held. It was one big emotional moment for Rita and all her friends. Ashwini's daughter would be leaving society forever. She was like a kid to all. But this episode once again brought all the friends together.

They all were involved in all the facility management activities for the event, handling guests and family members.

One day Divya came to Rita's house, and she looked quite upset. She could not bear any further taunts from her sons and wanted to share the property equally among them. Rita asked her never to do so. She explained, 'The sons of yours come to see you at least once just in greed of the wealth & property you possess. Once you have given them all, they would never look after you. At such an old age, you may require the support of your kids. But to remove their anxiousness, make a legal will dividing the property equally among your sons after your death.' Rita knew a lawyer very well and she connected with him to speak to Divya. In just a week the document was ready. Divya happily shared the same with her sons. Both were satisfied as now they knew what they would get after their mother's demise. They could not do much to it, as anyways the documents cannot be altered until and unless Divya decides to do so. The solution worked and now there was no more mental harassment inflicted by her sons on Divya.

Everything was quite smooth in Rita's life. But age was catching up. She remained ill due to high sugar and blood pressure. Her son and daughter would often visit her and take her for regular checkups. One day Rita while doing some household chores suddenly fell to the ground and lost her sense. It was good that the mattress was laid on the ground because of which she did not receive any grave physical injury. Also luckily, the housemaid was present when this incident occurred. Immediately she informed all her friends in society. They hurriedly called the ambulance and informed her kids. Both took the very next flight to the city. The doctor did a thorough check-up and found out that Rita was suffering from an advanced level of spondylitis. It took almost a week to recover from the same. The situation has changed a lot, as Rita's son was not ready to leave her alone in the house. Even Rita remained quite shaky after the whole incident. She too had lost confidence in her. There was a clear understanding that now she cannot leave single-handedly in the house. The doctor had clearly said that the same situation can get repeated. The biggest pain for her was that her son was requesting to sell the house. He could not take care of the building due to his busy schedule back at his work location. Neither they wanted to rent it out as last time, the tenant had done big damage to the 1st floor one bedroom-kitchen room that was allotted to him for a year. After he left, the walls had to be completely painted as the kid of the occupant had drawn pictures with pen & pencils everywhere. The house cannot be left vacant for long as there were chances of robbery and thefts in the area.

Rita had shared this with a few of her friends. They were shocked and unhappy with the decision but they knew that it was inevitable. They all were growing old and they needed some kind of support system. It would be a wise and sensible choice to stay with their kids. Through some word-of-mouth publicity, a few people started showing interest in buying the house. The location of building was at a prime area, although it needed a complete overhaul and makeover. In just two weeks, a very lucrative offer came and the deal was done.

It was a very sad moment for Rita. She was about to leave the house that was so dear to her. In addition to that, she must part with her lifelong friends. The same night she could not sleep. All those memories with her hubby and kids accumulated in the house kept flashing before her wide-open eyes. The feeling was as if someone has squeezed the whole blood out of her body. This went on for a few nights. Somehow, she had consoled and readied herself for the big day. Finally, after a few days, she registered the building in the name of the new owner. All formalities were done and there was just one day with her to stay in society in her house. Her friends planned a farewell ceremony for her in the evening. It was quite an emotional and nerve-wracking situation for Rita. She was garlanded with flowers and a shawl on arrival. Her friends asked her to give a parting speech for which she was not ready at all. But then she had to.

'Dear Friends. You never want to leave your pals ever in your lifetime. It is one of the relations that you make by choice. You nurture it every day. I was lucky to have you all in my life. After the sudden death of my husband, you all created an invisible rock support system for me. It was because of you all that I could live and manage alone in this house. But every product and relation has an expiry. The time has come when I must leave you all and settle down with my son in another city. It would be quite difficult for me. I got habituated to having my afternoon tea with all of you. Conversing with you every day had become a part of my daily chore. I will miss you all a lot. Will try to be in touch with each one of you through calls and messages.'

Rita's voice had turned cold and she was shivering. Her eyes were teary which further prevented her from speaking any further. The entire room was silent. Just the sound of sobbing could be heard from all corners. Everybody was crying. Rita's son too looked visibly disturbed. He could feel the pain his mother and her friends were going through. The experience was quite heartbreaking and sad. Sometimes you take practical decisions in life as you do not have any other options left. Though it hurts you, still you take those harsh steps. Nothing is permanent, change is constant.

!!!

2 AM Friend

Gaurav was a very social guy always surrounded by lots and lots of friends. As he was born and brought up in a joint family, he was accustomed to sharing and caring for people in and around him. He was a lucky go person who was very flexible and adjustable in all kinds of environments. He did not carry any air and was very approachable & friendly with everyone. The only two areas where he as a person failed were, that he trusted people easily, and secondly, his expectations from his friends were always very high. This always created a strain in terms of any person he encountered as he believed in giving his best in the association. But if the reciprocation from the other individual was not as per his hopes, then it created a lot of frustration in him. Due to this reason, he was not able to make any good pal who would stand as a big support for him whenever he required. He neither does have a 2 am kind of friend to whom he can call at any point in time to share any issue or problem. Fate has not been kinder to him whenever it came to making a lifetime kind of companion in his existence.

Mohit, the other character of this story was the kind of person who was very reserved and believed in keeping his things to himself. Born in a nuclear family, where his mother was a school teacher and his father worked in a local factory, the atmosphere in his house always remained tense. He did not share a very cordial relationship with his dad. This might be a perception but that is what he believed in. He always felt that his dad loved his sister more than him. This made a big impact on the nature of the poor guy as he lacked confidence, was quite aggressive, and always carried a bad temper. Due to this, he too was not able to make one such good friend whom he could call his dearest comrade.

Gaurav and Mohit were in the same class. But in their early childhood, they rarely interacted with each other. The reason being even though they were in the same class, in the same school, and the same town but their houses were quite a distance from each other and the buses on which they traveled were also separate and followed different routes to reach the school.

Destiny had a plan for them as by luck in Standard 9, Gaurav started traveling to school in the same bus in which Mohit used to commute. It so happened that Gaurav's father's company in the initial days provided a company bus for all children as an extra benefit to employees but recently it suffered huge financial losses and thus all these facilities got withdrawn. This became a blessing for both the mate as their friendship started blossoming with period and they got to spend time in each other's company. Every day in the evening Mohit would come to Gaurav's house and there they would play cricket; one would be a bowler and the other would be at the batting crease. Rest they never felt the requirement of a third person as they would cap on the roles of the fielder, the wicketkeeper, and the empire by themselves.

###################

The best times that they spent were during festivals, especially during the Durga puja which was celebrated with high fanfare and enthusiasm in the town. Both would request their parents for 20 or 30 rupees which they would spend on delicious local snacks like Phuckas, Jalebis, samosa, etc. (Indian snacks) which were beautifully displayed in the stalls very near to the area where the deity of Goddess was placed in the central area of the plot. Aside from that, many other shops for food, jewelry, cosmetics, dresses, games, etc. were set up at the location for 7-8 days so that all the families could enjoy the festive occasion. For one complete week, 20 or 30 rupees was a very minuscule amount but both friends knew the limitation of their parents. Thus, they remained more than happy with the pocket money received from their elders. On one such day, a very funny incident occurred, as when they were eating 'Samosa', there was a power cut for 2 minutes. The moment electricity came back, Gaurav noticed that Mohit was picking up the 'Samosa' from the ground which unfortunately had slipped from his plate. This was hilarious for Gaurav but embarrassing for Mohit, though they laughed heartily for the next 1 hour, and the rest of their lives, this remained as an evergreen memory inscribed in their hearts. But this is how childhood is as with limited money, sometimes you compromise on things which for the elderly would sound quite stupid. Nevertheless, they both damn cared about what other people were thinking about them and enjoyed every bit of the moment.

####################

Mohit and Gaurav had two more friends in the town, Jyoti, and Deepika and all four were part of the same tuition class (Mishra Sir who used to teach Mathematics and Physics).

After school hours they spent around 4 hours together having lunch, attending classes, and then finally traveling back home. Most of the time they would catch a local bus as the way back journey home from tuition was almost 10km but sometimes they remained lucky as Jyoti's father was senior professional and many times they used to get a free ride in a car or jeep for ferrying. On one such occasion, while they all were returning home by bus, a guy aged around 20-22 years hopped up on the bus. He was tall, dark with spectacles in his eyes carrying a very serious expression on his face. He was continuously staring at Jyoti and Deepika as if he knew them. The perplexed faces of both the girls brought a smile to Mohit and seeing him smiling, Gaurav too started making funny looks. This gradually brought laughter to the entire group and for the rest of the journey (an hour), they all kept on giggling. This annoyed the young lad but he kept quiet the entire period. Once the bus had stopped at the bus station and all of them de-boarded the vehicle, the young lad caught Mohit by Collar and started threatening him.

Young Lad: Hey why were you all laughing at me? Do you think I am a joker?

Mohit: Leave my collar first and do not try to bully me. It is of no use. (He turned almost red in anger).

Young Lad: First tell me what was so funny that kept you entertained for so long.

Mohit: Nothing, but if you insist then I must say you look so comical.

The tempers flared up and very soon it could have worsened into a full-blown fight. The girls pushed Gaurav to intervene.

Jyoti: Gaurav, what kind of friend you are? See Mohit seems to be in trouble and you are standing here like a statue.

Finally, Gaurav intervened and asked the young lad to take it easy as they all were laughing at a joke that was cracked by one of the girls and they never intended to offend him. After a few more hot verbal exchanges, the young lad finally loosened his grip on Mohit's collar and he left the place. The girls cursed Gaurav for being clumsy as he wasted 10 minutes, he should have pacified the person a bit early. Gaurav and Mohit were cool about it as both found the incident very amusing.

Gaurav just said to the girls that they do not need to worry about Mohit as he is like our legendary and courageous king Prithviraj Chauhan who never backed off from his enemy's challenges. He was never dependent on anyone for any help as he is a one-man army. Hearing this, once again the entire group burst into laughter.

################

There was one more incident wherein Mohit picked up a fight with a boy who was saying something wrong about Gaurav and his family. It so happened that one day while both friends were strolling late in the evening, a boy passed by wearing a skin-tight shirt and pants. He was looking hilarious and both the friends started laughing at seeing him. This infuriated the boy and he started abusing Gaurav and his family. Mohit could not take it and he hit the boy very hard on his face. Later he pushed him with full force which made the boy fall flat on the road. Gaurav got terrified seeing Mohit's aggressive approach. He tried his best to separate the boy from the grip of

Mohit. At one point in time, it seemed that he would almost kill the chap. Once he released the youth from Mohit's hands, he asked the person to run away as soon as possible. Though he was proud that his friend stood by him but then tried to explain to him that he should not have taken the fight as there were ways by which they could have taught a good lesson to the boy. This incident made the bond between both friends stronger.

In the New Year, Mohit and Gaurav had planned that they would stay awake together till midnight. Both friends told their respective parents that they would be doing late-night study at a friend's place and then left their respective houses. Both roamed freely on the cold freezing breezy winter night of 31st December in the lonely streets of the town casually. At midnight they felt that they should do something interesting to make this first outing a memorable one. Gaurav was the naughty one, wickedly he pointed out toward the street lights. A cunning smile flashed on the faces of both the boys, they started picking stones and aiming at the glittering tube lights. One, two, three they missed their targets by inches. Finally, Mohit made the first breakthrough by hitting the street light precisely. A loud deafening noise of glass echoed through the surrounding. They felt an instant shivering through the spine for some time out of excitement and fear. It was a densely populated area with many houses around. Instead of backing out, they started aiming at those lights with full vigor, and one by one both broke around five of them. Suddenly, they heard the footsteps of people coming in the same direction as theirs. This scared the hell out of them. Both ran like a rabbit that is being chased by some wild dog and in no time, they had covered two kilometers in just a few minutes. They looked at each other and laughed for a while. Lather they hugged & wished each other a very happy new year.

############

With time, they both grew into young teen lads where the attraction for the opposite sex grows naturally. Mohit was the first one who fell in love with a girl called Priyanka who was in the same class as where he was. There were three challenges, number one he was very shy to express his feelings to her, number two he was scared as his mother was a teacher in the same school, and three he lacked confidence as she was too good at studies whereas Mohit was an average guy. He shared his feelings with Gaurav who got a bit surprised at first but then decided to help him. Both chalked out a plan where Gaurav would request their close friend Deepika to help them out as she was a good friend of Priyanka. So, one fine day Gaurav went to Deepika's house with a strategized pre-plan.

Deepika: Hi, Gaurav. How are you?

Gaurav: I am good. I have a plan for us concerning our studies.

Deepika: What plan Gaurav?

Gaurav: See, as our exams are approaching, we all could do group studies. As you are good at mathematics, you could help us three and as I am ok with Literature, I can guide you all. Similarly, Mohit and Jyoti can help us in Chemistry and Biology which is their core strength.

Deepika: That is a great idea.

Gaurav was trying his best to change the topic and come to the actual point. Things were not happening as to what he had planned to execute. Somehow, he was losing his confidence but then finally mustered all his strength and spoke to her.

Gaurav: Deepika, I wanted to speak about something related to Mohit.

Deepika: Why, what happened? Is everything ok with Mohit?

Gaurav: Yes, he is fine, just that he is a bit confused nowadays. He looks very sad and lost in some kind of thought.

Deepika: Why are you baffling me, Gaurav? Tell me clearly what is going on with Mohit.

Gaurav with a very sober face and serious tone started again.

Gaurav: He has started liking someone.

Deepika: What do you mean by liking someone? Even if he has started liking someone, then what is wrong with it? We all like each other, aren't we?

Gaurav: Oh! You do not understand what I mean.

Deepika: Tell me no. You are testing my patience now.

Gaurav: Ok, he has started liking Priyanka and he wants that you convey his feeling to her.

The moment she heard it, her facial expression changed. She could not believe her ears and she reacted as if she has heard something which is out of this world.

Deepika: Wait for a second. Do you mean that Mohit likes Priyanka? Is he mad or what?

Gaurav: It is quite normal Deepika for a boy to like a girl. He loves her.

Deepika: I never thought that Mohit is such a kind of guy. This is not happening and I do not like these all things. It is not the right time for all these craps.

For a minute, Gaurav became nervous as Deepika's families were family friends and their parents occasionally met each other. He started imagining what would happen if Deepika shares this incident with her mother and by any chance, if his mother comes to know about it, he would be thrown out of the house. The very thought left him to tremble with fear and thus he made a U-Turn. He never expected such a strong reaction from her. Thus, he opted for an escapist plan.

Gaurav: Really, I too am ashamed of Mohit. I do not know what to say. It is just that I was feeling very bad about it and wanted to share the same with a trusted friend like you. I do not want to remain his pal. For sure, from tomorrow onwards I would stop talking to him and cut all relations. He is a very stupid guy.

Deepika: Right.

Gaurav: Deepika, do not tell these things to Aunty, ok?

Deepika: Ok but then explain to Mohit to stop all these nonsensical things.

Gaurav: Sure. Have a good day. Bye for now.

Hastily he returned and the very next day met Mohit. Mohit was too excited to hear the outcome of the discussion.

Mohit: Hi bro. Hope our mission is accomplished and Deepika is ready to be our partner in crime.

Gaurav: Hmm. I think you should back off or think of some alternative way as she got very irate on hearing all the stuff. She was very angry with you.

Mohit's face turned pale as first love is always very special. This was the end of the love story of Mohit and it got finished even before getting started. Cleverly Gaurav did not disclose the entire episode wherein he told Deepika that he would disassociate himself from Mohit.

###############

One more comical event was when the entire 10th class went for a picnic. Both Gaurav and Mohit were excited about this and were busy imagining the fun they would have on the trip. It started all well when the students gathered at the school premises where a bus had come that was supposed to take them to their destination. The entire journey on the bus was overtly enjoyable as both boys and girls danced as if it was the end of the world. All popular songs were played, and even the teachers who were part of this trip joined in the frolic moment.

As soon as they reached the spot, the entire batch was mesmerized by the beauty of the location. A view of the Rocky Mountains with the flowing river beside it added to the beauty of the place. They divided themselves into smaller groups so that they could unwind and explore the exquisiteness of the site. It so happened that Mohit and Gaurav were accompanied by four girls and two boys. Among them was a girl named Aruna. She kept on staring at Gaurav for an unknown reason and at one point in time he finally out of curiosity asked her.

Gaurav: Aruna, am I looking so handsome today that your eyes are completely focused on me since the beginning of this trip?

Aruna: Shut up Gaurav. It is just that your T-shirt is looking fabulous and I feel like buying one for myself.

Gaurav: Oh, hello Miss Aruna. You will not get another piece anywhere in India as this has been gifted to me by my sister from a shop that only keeps unique sets of clothing with them.

Aruna: Ok. Sorry but the design of the outfit is mind-blowing. Good luck hero.

Gaurav was surprised to get such cheesy comments from his friend but then he was happy to see that his dress is allowing him to get some sort of attention.

When he returned after the wonderful picnic, he thanked his elder sister for the T-Shirt. Her sister revealed that this does not belong to her and she has borrowed it from one of her hostel mates. Also, she remarked that the same girl is the elder sister of one of your friends in your class named Aruna.

For a second, he just could not believe his ears and was in utter shock. He recollected the entire day's event and all the discussions he had with Aruna concerning the T-shirt.

He turned red with shame as he realized that he was continuously boasting about a dress to Aruna which belonged to her elder sister.

He narrated the entire episode to her sister and she laughed her heart out. For the next two months, Gaurav stopped looking at Aruna out of embarrassment but thanked her silently every day for keeping this secret to herself and saving him from a very major awkwardness.

################

The most emotional moment in their life came when both Mohit and Gaurav got their farewell from junior class before their 10th board exam. They both had tears in their eyes as they knew that post this exam, both will have to tread on a different journey.

After the farewell, they sat till 10 pm on the same ground where they met every day to play cricket. Both reminisced all the good old golden days when they had jolly merry moments. They went to Jyoti and Deepika's houses also to wish them good luck with the exams. The girls were also grief-stricken as they were such an inseparable group that stood with each other at all odds.

#################

Post their board exam; both friends got separated for a little period as Mohit got admitted to a college whereas Gaurav joined a school that had 11th and 12th classes academics on its campus. They started spending less time with each other as they got busy with the curriculum and new environment of the novel place. Both made a fresh set of friends but they remained connected. After separation, instead of the bond getting weaker, they got closer to each other. On weekends either Mohit would come down to Gaurav's house or Gaurav would visit his friend's place. Sometimes they would meet at the same playground where they had spent their entire childhood enjoying, quarreling, or teasing each other. Very soon the festival of color, Holi was to arrive and both planned that this time they would have a ball of a time together. They bought different colors for the same and deliberated to meet all the old friends near their home. On Holi, there is a strong tradition that you take the blessings of your elders by sprinkling a kind of hue on their feet. Mohit politely did the same to Gaurav's parents and his elder sister, post which both the friends moved out to celebrate the occasion with the rest of their pals. On the way, whomever they met, both made a point to splash them with all the beautiful colors that they were carrying with them. While both were busy enjoying the festival, suddenly Gaurav recalled something that made him exclaim.

Gaurav: Bro let us go to Sohan's place. I have heard that he makes grand arrangements at his place. There happens a lot of dancing, eating, drinking, and playing.

Mohit: That is a nice idea. Come on let us go there.

Sohan was two years older than them and had studied in the same school from where both had passed out. He was very friendly and jovial to both friends.

True to the expectation, they found many people gathered at the place. A beautiful tent was set out where many water-filled colored buckets were laid out in open, and people were filling the water guns from them and sprinkling on the faces and bodies of each other. Trays of sweets were lying in the corner unattended as all were busy enjoying the beautiful festival. A DJ was playing fantastic songs of 'Holi' from Bollywood movies and all were dancing to the tune of the same. Overall, the sight was very eye catchy and pleasant.

Sohan welcomed both by hugging and patting the back, expressing his happiness at their arrival.

Sohan: So, how are you two?

Mohit: Fine. It seems we are in a different exotic land.

Gaurav: Not an exotic land, but rather a different planet altogether.

All of them laughed heartily.

Sohan: You are right but allow me to serve you a majestic drink that you will remember for a lifetime.

Both Mohit and Gaurav were curious & excited to taste the beverage. Sohan poured the juice into larger earthen glassware to the top of the brim and asked them to have it. Gaurav was a bit nervous and to make sure that they are not consuming anything which they might regret later, he sheepishly asked Sohan.

Gaurav: What is the content of this drink? I mean, I hope that it will not harm us in any way.

Sohan: Come on! Why would I offer you something which is not safe? Ok, wait.

Sohan had a glass of beverage in front of them to prove that all is well.

Seeing that, Mohit insisted Gaurav have it.

Mohit: Gaurav why are you so anxious? It seems you are reading a lot of crime series nowadays. Let us have it, bro. It looks delicious.

Mohit and Gaurav took the first sip. Wow, it was yummier than what they had expected. Milk with lots of cashew nuts, raisins, almonds, and fruits like grapes, bananas, etc. mixed in it. They gulped down the entire glass of drink in a second. Now they were requesting one more round. Sohan filled their respective glasses and the two friends consumed the same in another minute.

Mohit requested one more glass but then Sohan refused same.

Sohan: No, I cannot give you one.

Mohit: But why? You have a drum full of the beverage.

Sohan: No, means no.

This raised the eyebrows of both friends.

Sohan: Guys this drink consisted of a local paste of the ground leaves and flowering tops of cannabis.

Gaurav: Did not get you. What is cannabis?

Sohan: It is a mild intoxicating paste of a leaf. So more than two glasses can be harmful and that's why now you two should leave for your houses.

Mohit and Gaurav took the advice of Sohan very lightly as instead of heading towards their home; they sat under the shade of a nearby banyan tree. After 15-20 minutes they felt their head swinging and they started feeling dizzy. They stared at each other for a while as if to reassure each other that all is well but all was not ok.

Gaurav: Bro, I am feeling sleepy and my vision is also getting blurred. Am I looking normal?

Mohit: What are you saying, bro? I am also feeling a bit dizzy.

A dog passed by them and seeing the canine Gaurav started laughing uncontrollably.

Mohit: Bro, what is the matter with you? What is making you laugh?

Gaurav: Can't you see the tail of the dog?

Mohit: Yes, I can see that. But what is so funny about it?

Gaurav: It is completely twisted and looks abnormal.

Saying this Gaurav once again started laughing hysterically and fell to the ground with his hands on his stomach. A minute later Mohit too began giggling and chuckling, so much that people started looking at them with weird looks. For another 10 minutes, it was a complete laugh riot and none of them were able to stop tittering.

Both understood that they had consumed something which is making them lose their senses. Gaurav with an expression conveyed that he is leaving for his house immediately. Instantly Mohit too left for his parent's place.

Gaurav, on reaching his house straightaway opened the TV set to divert his mind. His sister arrived in the drawing room where the electronic device was kept and sat beside his brother. Suddenly Gaurav started crying which amazed his sister as she was not able to understand what triggered his brother to sob. Seeing his brother weeping, she became a bit worried and asked him the reason for being so sad. He kept mum and continued looking at the ground. Finally, he confessed that he had consumed some intoxicating drink and that his emotions are not under his control. Hearing this, his sister asked him to immediately take bath and then take a nice nap before anyone especially their parents come to know about it. Instantly Gaurav left for the shower. While he poured a mug of water over his head, he felt as if he is swimming in a vast ocean where fishes are spinning, whirling & swaying by his side. Out of fear, he quickly started taking bath and completed the same in another few minutes. Later when he rolled down over the bed to take sleep, he started hallucinating as if he is in heaven surrounded by various Gods and Goddesses who are welcoming him into the new world. He tightly kept his eyes closed so that no scarier thoughts come to his mind. After half an hour he fell asleep and woke after six-hour of continuous dozing.

On the other hand, when Mohit reached his house, he promptly asked his mother to serve food as he was feeling hungry. Normally his intake is low in the afternoon but today he was having an abnormal diet. His mother could not comprehend and was not able to believe what she was seeing. She was happy to see his son feeding on all the dishes passionately. Post his lunch Mohit too directly ran towards the bathroom to take a bath where he nearly spent an hour daydreaming and recalling all the chapters of History subject where he could see different kings and queens sitting beside him discussing, plotting, and planning to attack the neighboring regions. He too took a 7-hours sound sleep which again was not normal.

After this event, both friends pledged henceforth that they would never take such kind of mind-altering drink again and would never trust anyone who influences them to do so.

###############

With time, the aspirations, desires, and wishes of both pals started taking newer twists and turns. While Gaurav put his entire focus on his academics, Mohit's attention moved on to a girl who studied in the same college of which he was part. He fell in love with the lady and she too reciprocated in the same fashion. Their lovey-dovey affair was the most talked-about hot discussion in the university. Their pairing was considered too cute in the eyes of all their fellow mates. This also drew the unwanted attention of a few unscrupulous boys who were ill-mannered and behaved nastily with girls. Among them was Vishu who would knowingly keep on passing spiteful and mean comments on the couple. This irritated Mohit a lot and one fine day he went to discuss the same with him.

Mohit: Vishu what is your problem? Why do you pass unpleasant lewd remarks on me and my girlfriend?

Vishu: (With a vicious smile on his face) You don't deserve her.

Mohit: What do you mean by that I don't deserve her?

Vishu: See my personality dude. I should be her boyfriend as she is worthy of a boy like me as I am more handsome, sorted, and clear in my thoughts.

Mohit's blood started boiling in anger and in a moment of heat, he pushed Vishu with both hands.

Every action has an equal and opposite reaction. Vishu gathered himself up and gave a tight punch to Mohit on his nose. Blood started oozing out of his nose profusely and for another 5 minutes, he lay on the ground silently. A few students took him to the medical room where he was given first aid. Meanwhile, Vishu had vanished and fled from the spot.

Mohit was completely disturbed by this incident and he wanted to take revenge on Vishu. He discussed this with Gaurav who tried to reason him out.

Gaurav: Mohit, forget it, bro. This happens and neither you nor Vishu was wrong. It just happened and you should move on as I don't think Vishu will ever again try to come your way.

Mohit: Are you trying to say that I should spare that idiotic person? It seems you don't want to support me; you are a coward.

Gaurav understood that it was of no use to explain anything to Mohit now as he is in a fit of rage and probably he needs to give some more time to Mohit to rethink.

Gaurav: OK fine, take 2 days and let me know as to what you plan to do actually. You will always find me by your side.

Mohit: Ok

After 2 days Mohit asked Gaurav to meet him at their favorite place, the local playground.

Mohit: Bro, I have decided and I am not going to leave that guy so easily. See Vishu takes a particular route to the college, and most of the time he travels all alone on his bike. So, we can catch him somewhere on the way. I just want to hit him hard so that he remembers the same for his entire lifetime.

Gaurav: But what if he is accompanied by 1-2 batch mates?

Mohit: Oh! I never thought of it.

Gaurav: Do not worry, I will ask Bappi and Bombi to join us as a back- up.

Mohit: Are you talking about those 2 drug addicts? I think you have lost your mind.

Gaurav: Then who do you think will join us for such a highly saintly activity planned by you? (Gaurav got a bit irritated) Aside from that their services will not be free buddy and we will have to pay them for the same.

Mohit: Hmm. As you say.

Gaurav: See I will arrange that but you need to promise me one thing.

Mohit: What?

Gaurav: We will only teach Vishu a lesson by just frightening him with 2-3 punches. You will not cross the limit.

Mohit: Ok, I promise.

The stage was set and all 4 camped near the road on the said date eagerly waiting for Vishu to pass by. The college used to start at 9 am and Vishu used to cross the route at 8:45 am. So, they had reached the spot by 8 am only. The clock moved at its own pace but Mohit was waiting impatiently for Vishu to arrive. Soon it reached 8:45, then 9:00, and finally 10:00 but there was no sign of the guy. They waited for another hour but had no luck.

Mohit: I think he might not be coming today

Gaurav: It seems destiny is with him currently. So, Mohit what should be our next move bro?

Mohit: Can we come here again tomorrow?

Gaurav: Come on Mohit, forget it. Move on chap as you will not get anything by taking vengeance. But next time if Vishu messes with you unnecessarily, I would be the first person to join you in hitting him left and right.

Mohit: Hmm.

Mohit was disappointed and dismayed but agreed with what Gaurav was trying to explain. On the other hand, Gaurav took a sigh of relief as he had never been in favor of violence. He was scared that their wrong activity might reach the ears of their parents. Fate was in his favor this time

###############

With time both friends got busy in their respective lives but then they made a point to meet whenever the time permitted them to do so. One such occasion was the marriage of Gaurav's elder sister which was supposed to happen in a remote location, the original hometown of Gaurav. Both mates were young studying in the 2nd year of graduation and were completely unaware of the nitty-gritty of Indian weddings. When Gaurav asked Mohit to attend the wedding, without a second thought he packed his bag and reached the location.

Seeing his friend, Gaurav took a sigh of relief as he needed his help desperately on various work assigned to him by his father. Two more friends, Vijay and Sherpa too had come to attend the wedding and support Gaurav. Crucial jobs like catering arrangement, lighting, flower decoration, banquet booking, etc. were the few odd works whose onus lay on the shoulder of Gaurav. Mohit accompanied him to all the places and never left his friend alone. Together they both slowly and gradually completed all their task and waited for the final D-day when the Groom's family was supposed to arrive in the town. It was supposed to reach the community hall first in the morning and then at the night, a marriage procession of the Groom along with all his friends & family would reach the bride's residence where the nuptial rites and rituals would take place. It so happened that just the night before, one more wedding had happened at the hall and they left the place in a very shabby condition. However, Gaurav's father employed a few blue-collared workers to clean all the rooms and gallery of the hall, yet the pungent smell of rotten food engulfed the area. Also, the water arrangement at the location was not up to the mark as due to some reason the water was not available 24*7. Thus, the process of collecting and filling tubs via an emergency water tanker was becoming a tedious job.

Gaurav and Mohit gave their best as they stayed at the hall till 3 am decorating the area with pleasant-smelling flora and spraying lots of room fresheners to moderate the strong bitter odor surrounding the hall. Mattresses, bed sheets, pillows, and a thin blanket were put across the place. Different rooms were allotted for men and women where they could spend their time comfortably. Mohit stayed back at the location while Gaurav left for the house to have a short nap as he was supposed to cross-check other arrangements also.

Early in the morning around 8 am, the Groom family was at the community hall. Surprisingly all the beautiful aroma had vanished in the morning and the same old nasty foul smell encircled the entire region. The guests were quite upset about it which was easily palpable on their faces. Mohit started trembling with fear as people started grilling him with questions about the facilities readied at the place. The acute shortage of running water flared the tempers of people. There was no senior around and so Mohit frantically called his friend Gaurav and updated him about the situation. Meanwhile, the invitees threatened to vacate the location and this made Mohit quite nervous. Tears started rolling down his eyes as he was feeling terrible about the entire episode. His tiny shoulder could not handle the pressure anymore. Meanwhile, Gaurav and his father with a few more relatives reached the spot and hurriedly took control of the situation. One more water tanker got assigned to the place and lots of flowers with fragrances were deployed at the hall. Soon the situation became normal and breakfast was served to all with a cup of hot tea. A few ladies from the bride's side too arrived to take care of the female guests. All in all, the tense environment visible a few minutes back had turned into a relaxed situation where only happy faces were noticeable around.

In the evening, the marriage procession of the groom arrived at the bride's house with lots of pomp and fare. All the friends of Gaurav danced along with the crowd and had a ball of the time. The marriage occurred with no more untoward incident and the girl was given a farewell with a happy and sober heart.

############################

With time, the charm in the relationships fades away but that was not the case with the friendship of Mohit and Gaurav. They stayed connected and kept the bond going more strongly. After graduation, both friends joined different companies as per their interests and professional arena. Both became quite busy in their work as now they had something to prove to the world. Due to this, interaction among them almost became negligible. New workplace friends became part of their lives which was quite natural but the sense of attachment with them was always lacking.

Both friends once again got a chance to meet up. This was when Gaurav was getting married to the love of his life. Along with Mohit, Vijay an old childhood friend too came along to attend the ceremony. The two friends danced like wild fanatics in the wedding procession.

Unfortunately, a year later Gaurav was not present in Mohit's marriage but made it a point to visit his friend's house after the birth of her daughter. He also attended Mohit's sister's marriage.

However strong relation is, winds of misunderstanding and confusion can create a stir in the lives of people. Open discussions, well-being feelings for each other, social attachment, and maturity is the only secret to a happy relationship. Friends are people who bring a smile to your life as they don't judge you like office colleagues or people who do not know you properly. It requires special effort to balance and sustain a happy lifetime bond.

Purposefully I had mentioned the title of this story as "2 AM Friend" as I strongly believe that people should have one such friend in their lives to whom they can call and share their feelings at any odd hour of the day. Once you have such a friend treasure your relationship and understanding till you say goodbye to this materialistic world.

!!!

Support

Raman was patiently listening to all the instructions his boss was giving to drive the financial year target. After an hour's call, finally, his senior hung up the phone. The revenue numbers given to him were huge, almost double what he used to do every month. He knew that if he can achieve it, he would get a nice appraisal. He has been accomplishing all the goals in the current financial year consistently month on month. Raman did not want to falter in the end, thus immediately he called up a meeting for his team members at the zonal office. Five business development managers (BDM) used to report to him directly and then there were other cross-functional members whose dotted reporting was assigned to him like trainers, product advisors, and the local HR team member.

The key lay in driving and pushing his five BDMs who had the experience of delivering the output when required the most. They all had arrived on time for the most awaited gathering of the year. Raman had knowingly put up a very serious face so that everyone understands the gravity of the situation. With a straight face, he started the conference.

Raman: Guys, this month, we will have to work a bit harder as the target assigned by the boss is quite high.

1st BDM: What is the target given?

Raman: One Crore revenue per BDM.

2nd BDM: What? This is just double what we do every month.

3rd BDM: This is not done. How will we be able to do this? It means we are not going to get our incentives this month.

4th BDM: How did you accept this unreasonable target?

5th BDM: I think this is an opportunity for all of us. We should gun for it. Super boss believes that as a team we can deliver.

So many questions from the workforce were disheartening for him. He knew that extracting the output expected by management would be a tedious job. But he was imagining some excitement from his team. In this case, 4 out of 5 of his team members were doubtful. When everyone was raising queries, the 5th BDM (seniormost BDM) put an optimistic remark. It was kind of relief for him. Taking a page out of words spoken by everyone, Raman started to speak.

Raman: Great, that is what I wanted to hear. Some negative remarks, apprehensions, doubts, and finally someone who thinks that this would be a huge prospect for us. Team, believe me, this is a great chance to prove our worth as a team. The appraisal is scheduled for next month, and triumphing the numbers will enable a better outlook for each one of us.

3rd BDM: What if we are not able to break the ceiling?

Raman: Nothing, no one is going to crucify us for not attaining our targets. We will still gain respect from the entire ecosystem for trying something which looks impossible as of now. Also, I guarantee each one of you that your appraisal will not get impacted by just this month's achievement.

The final wordings of Raman gave stability to the anxious minds of his team members. They felt more relaxed and self-assured now. Now they all sat down to plan how they can hit the bull's eye. The brainstorming session lasted for 2 more hours in which all probabilities and possibilities were deliberated. Ultimately, they chalked out a strategy to reach the breakeven point. They divided partners into 3 categories A, B, and C. Each set will be monitored and provided with a scheme according to their investment and billing capability. In case, they miss any number, they will keep a few partners aligned as a backup who could bill more than what is decided initially. Marketing support and end consumer discount were also decided which were required to get the required number. Once everything was strategized, the team had a cocktail dinner together. At the same place, their stay was arranged as the party went on till late at night. Early morning, they all left for their respective work locations.

For the next 30 days, the team worked day and night to achieve an incredible task. Finally, together they justified the popular saying, **"Where there is a will, there is a way"**. Not only did they achieve it but crossed the same by a margin of 10% above the required number.

The boss was ecstatic, he called up Raman to congratulate him for his fantabulous effort. He further asked him,

Boss: Raman, you are the most efficient colleague ever I have worked with. Tell me, what can I do for you to elate your career growth?

Raman: Sir, thank you. First, this was not possible without your support and team contribution. Still, if you feel that I am worth enough, then allow me to manage the North region.

Boss: Hmm, it means you want to work at headquarters. Aren't you scared that even I too be based out of the same office in Delhi?

Raman: Sir, I would get better insights and inputs from you if I stay near you. No risk, no gain. (There was some sort of mischief in the way he spoke these lines).

Boss: Ok, so you find me a risky person to work with (with a chuckle). Give me some time and I will get back to you.

Even Raman could not stop his smile while hearing the sarcastic reply from his boss. (Good that his boss was not able to see him live).

One more month passed by, and Raman was getting restless as he desperately wanted to shift to Delhi. Currently, he was based out of Kolkata and was managing the Eastern region. The real reason was that his wife was posted in a Central Government school as a teacher in the capital city, Delhi. Thus, he was trying for a long to shift his base there. For him, this was the last hope. He had thought of changing the company if his request is put on hold this time.

Friendzzz

On one of the Friday mornings, while he was preparing the projection for the subsequent month, suddenly an e-mail popped up in his inbox. On seeing the subject line of the communication, 'Transfer Information', and on finding that the same has been initiated from HR, he got a bit curious. He immediately opened that mail to check the content. The matter in the correspondence was as below:

Dear Raman,

We are pleased to inform you that you have been transferred to Delhi with effect from 1st June. Your salary has been revised to $20000 per annum and the terms & conditions remain the same as per your initial joining letter.

You will have to give handover to Mr. Sayantan Dasgupta, in Kolkata who will take care of the east region from next week onwards. In Delhi, you will be briefed on your work scope by your reporting head Mr. Vinay Gupta (the name of his Boss).

We are looking forward to seeing more excellent work from you in your new location in the company. In case of any queries, please feel free to connect me.

Yours Sincerely

Aditi Sharma (Asst. HR Manager)

Raman was ecstatic out of excitement as he had waited for this for a long. On the very same day, he started readying for the handover as he just had one week left with him to leave for the new place. On the last day, he got an emotional farewell from his existing team members with a cake-cutting ceremony followed by a party in the evening organized by his colleagues. As a parting gift, he was presented with an official Blueberry Shirt and an evergreen Parker Pen.

Filled with sentiments, but eager to meet his wife and kids in Delhi, he gathered all his positive energies while leaving his favorite city Kolkata. On reaching Delhi, he spent some time with his family and then the next day reached the office to attend the meeting. He was a bit nervous as he will have to adapt to a new culture and work environment. Moreover, he will have to prove his worth to new team members. The session was to be addressed by boss Mr. Vinay Gupta and was mandatory for every team member of North to attend the same. As soon as he entered the room, the people were surprised to see a new unknown face. Just, when he was about to introduce himself to the crowd, from behind, the boss put a hand on his shoulder and with a smile addressed the team.

Boss: Good morning team. I am happy to announce that a new business head has joined the region, Mr. Raman. Raman had been instrumental in bringing lots of constructive changes in the East and now we want some of his expertise and guidance in bringing a turnaround in this region also with his vast knowledge of business expansion & market information. Over to you Raman, by the way, you are not allowed to fold the sleeves of your shirt in Delhi. This could have been possible in Kolkata but not here. Just be a bit cautious.

The way Boss passed on the sarcasm regarding his dress code made Raman a bit conscious about his overall presence. He felt a bit embarrassed as Boss could have shared the same thing one on one basis. But this is the moment of truth in the corporate world, expect the unexpected. Mustering all his strength, he took control of the situation and addressed the team members with complete confidence.

> Raman: Team, first, thanks to Boss for allowing me to lead this region. As per statistics, in major industries, 40% of revenue comes from the North region. For me, it is an honor and a great opportunity to lead the area. I assure you all that I would try my level best to support everyone in achieving organizational as well as individual goals. Before I delve into the business, I would request each one of you to explain to me the dynamics, opportunities, strengths, weaknesses, and threats of the trade of this location whenever I get a chance to meet you at your work sphere. Once again thanks to all of you for giving me a warm welcome.

The hall was filled with the din of claps and cheers. In the further course of time, planning and strategies were made by the boss along with the team. Raman just kept on observing as he knew that it will take some time to understand the dynamics of the region before he starts leading it full-fledged.

> After a few days, Raman planned a video call with all the BDMs of the North region as he knew that if he wants to stabilize himself in the new territory, then he will have to take this unit into control first. In the stipulated time, the entire team joined the call.

> Raman: Hi, team. I have gone through the data which shows that together as a team we have been delivering an

average monthly revenue of 2 crores. Boss has asked me to take this to 3 crores. He has also asked me to share the support required to reach this figure.

There was a pin-drop silence for a minute. It was finally broken by one of the BDM:

BDM 1: This is an imaginary number, impossible to achieve.

BDM 2: The management takes unilateral decisions; this is unacceptable.

BDM 3: The company does not take ground feedback before setting targets. How can we do such an incremental number in the lean season?

BDM 4: We are humans, not robots. Even if we work day and night, we will not be able to do it.

BDM 5: With such support, achieving 2 crores itself becomes a tedious task, how can someone ask for such revenue when they know that as a team, we are struggling to achieve the current number itself?

BDM 6: I think we can do it. If strategized properly, we can achieve our numbers easily.

Again, there was a pin-drop silence as out of 10 BDMs, someone had the guts to even think of the possibility of achieving the numbers. It was Subhash, the senior-most team member in the sales department who spoke amid all negativity. Subhash has seen so many ups and downs in the company and his life, that all herculean tasks seemed easy to him.

Raman was delighted to see someone being so optimistic and energetic. This gave him an extra dose of confidence which was very much required now. He started to speak.

Raman: Subhash, I am proud of you. We can discuss our plans in the next meeting. Just share with me the support part you all would require. In another hour I have a meeting with the boss where I need to share the same.

Subhash: We would require two things as support. First, a lucrative scheme for partners on purchase scheme. Second, a bombastic incentive for BDMs on achieving the target. If the same is as per our and market expectations, I promise you that we as a team would deliver.

Raman: Ok, give me some sort of rough idea as to what kind of scheme would work for both market and the team. I would try my level best to extract the same from the management.

The entire BDM team had a deep sense of respect for Subhash as he had helped each one of them in some or another way in stabilizing their job in the company. The team always backed him and his words were followed by the herd religiously. In just a few days Raman had understood this. He found a ray of hope in the dark & gloomy nights through the assuring words of Subhash. He was now more relaxed and secure as somewhere he has been accepted by Subhash and he knew that the rest of the BDMs would follow soon.

This was the beginning of an unsaid bond and friendship between Raman and Subhash. Although they were colleagues but treated each other like buddies outside the office campus.

There was one major challenge in front of Raman, coordination with other cross-functional teams especially, the training department. Trainers were led by a very shrewd guy Tapas who liked playing dirty politics in the system unnecessarily. Any request put by Raman regarding training needs was met with stiff resistance from him which was uncalled for. Raman was facing serious concerns regarding the training quality of the product advisor (sales team members placed at retail counters for the sale of the product. They reported to the BDMs). Due to inadequate knowledge and the absence of refresher training, the output from the team was getting poor day by day.

Raman shared this challenge with Subhash. Subhash then planned a way out and after in agreement with Raman, sent a mail to training head Tapas with a copy mark to all heads of departments regarding the pitiable quality of training in the system. He mentioned that due to a lack of proper product coaching, the sales of the product are getting impacted. This created quite a storm in the system as everybody knew that Subhash only highlights relevant issues. Quick actions were taken by Tapas and fresh training with proper schedules was shared with Raman. Tapas had to take affirmation on all the planned activities concerning the training of the product advisor from Raman. Raman was happy and he thanked Subhash heartily. From there on their friendship grew stronger.

Once Subhash fell ill and was diagnosed with dengue. The platelet count had reduced drastically and he needed blood infusion immediately. The chances of getting it became a difficult task as his blood group was AB+ which is considered very rare. Raman then immediately swung into action and contacted all blood donation hospitals, friends, family, and his complete colleague network. Luckily, one of his co-workers had the same group and he readily agreed to give the required quantity of blood required to save Subhash.

Slowly and gradually, both had developed a very strong brotherly link that could not be expressed in words. But then every relationship has a shelf life. Once Subhash required finance of 2 lacs rupees and he asked Raman for the same. Unfortunately, Raman did not have the money, and he stated his helplessness to Subhash. Initially, Subhash did not say anything but deep in his heart, he was hurt by the indifferent behavior of Raman. He felt that knowingly Raman had refused him for the money, whereas if tried sincerely he could have easily arranged the same.

A rift got created in their association. Raman was unaware of the reason why Subhash was angry with him but he could feel the coldness in Subhash's behavior. Subhash would not pick up his call after office hours, did not respond to messages, and in fact, he stopped meeting Raman at all friendly social gatherings. His gestures and conduct had become way too formal to be swallowed by Raman. So, one fine day he confronted Subhash;

Raman: Subhash, what has happened to you? You do not look normal.

Subhash: What abnormality did you see in me, Raman? All is fine. You are reading a lot between the lines.

Raman: (getting irritated) Do you think I am a fool, right? You do not want to spend time with me anymore, you do not want to speak with me the way you used to do earlier. Now you do not even revert to my messages. What is wrong with you? If there is something we need to discuss openly, then please do.

Subhash: There is no matter on which I want to have a conversation with you. You are assuming too much nowadays. All is well my friend. I have some urgent work to finish, so can I leave now?

Raman: (Angrily) Ok. Goodbye.

There was both sadness and furiousness in Raman's tone as he loved Subhash dearly. The cold expressions given by him were haunting Raman like anything. He kept his cool as he wanted to give sufficient time to Subhash as by now, somehow, he knew that he is not in a great mental state. Once he relaxes a bit, maybe he would speak to Subhash regarding his apathetic behavior.

Time & tide waits for none as the pressure of targets and revenue kept Raman busy. He also needed to give proper time to his family as his kid was very small and needed all his attention.

On one of the evenings, when he was about to just leave the office, a mail popped up on his official mail ID. It was from the legal team. The content was as mentioned below:

Friendzzz

Dear Raman,

We have received a legal notice from one of your partners who has claimed that he has been duped by one of your BDMs named Subhash concerning the scheme he was supposed to get in one of the purchases for January. He has mentioned that he was promised a lucrative benefit discount amount of around $7 on every single unit purchase. But he claims that he received only $5 per unit. Since he had done a purchase of 2000 units wherein, he should have gotten a benefit of $14000, but he had received $10000 only. So, there is a net loss of $4000. He has also stated that he has given many verbal and written reminders to Subhash but there is no revert from his end. All the emails and legal notices are attached for your kind reference.

Request to reply within the next 48 hours as this is a very sensitive issue that can defame the company's name and disrepute the ethical values that the organization stands for.

Yours Sincerely

Amit Kumar (Legal Department)

This was a very serious issue as the establishment was very strict and punitive concerning unfair ways of doing business. If proven guilty, an employee could be terminated on an immediate basis. Getting a sense of the criticality of the case, Raman called up Subhash immediately.

Raman: Subhash, just got a mail from the legal department. (He then explained the entire episode that had happened). What is the truth, Subhash? I want to know the real fact.

Subhash: I agree with whatever the partner has claimed. I have done the mistake under the pressure of the target and in greed for the incentive. In January there was a special scheme for employees for achieving 125% of the target. To achieve the same, I made false promises to the partner so that he bills the quantity I want him to do so.

Raman: But I have never seen you do this before. What made you do this?

Subhash: I was in dire need of money. I had taken a loan from someone who was threatening to return the money immediately or face consequences. Already the date on which I was to give the amount back had passed off.

Raman: Ok, but whatever you did was completely wrong. Let me think over it as to what could be done. You should have at least informed me once. I could have given you some sort of solution. Have you completely returned the loan amount by the incentive scheme you had earned or still something is due?

Subhash: Sorry Raman. Please save me. I did all this out of pressure. I have returned almost 70% of the money. Still, 30% of the amount remains unpaid.

Raman oscillated into action instantly. He spoke to the partner who had filed the case, who once again narrated the same story. He somehow convinced the channel partner to take back the legal case against Subhash and the organization if all his losses are covered by the institution within a scheduled period. The partner readily agreed as even he did not want to have a bad rapport with the company.

Raman had some financial authority wherein he could invest some amount in a partner for marketing purposes. As Subhash had committed based on overachievement done by the partner, Raman can take the liberty of giving the benefit to the channel partner. There were just two hurdles, first, the case was almost 4 months old, and second, the amount was on the higher side i.e., $4000 which needed approval from the boss. Somehow, he managed to convince his manager and provided the promised amount to the partner. The channel partner too immediately withdrew the case in good faith. It was a win-win situation for all.

The same evening Raman invited Subhash for a drink at the bar. He wanted Subhash to chill as he has gone through a tough phase in the recent past. Subhash too readily agreed to meet him. While they were having a fourth round of drinks, Subhash received a call from his lender. (The person from whom he had taken the loan).

Lender: Thanks, buddy. I have received the balance of 30% of the money today from one of your acquaintances. You did not return the amount on time but still, I am grateful to you for closing this transaction now.

Subhash: Hello, I really cannot understand what you are saying. I did not ask anyone to give back your money. Rather I was planning to come down to your house to discuss an extension date on the repayment of 30% of the pending loan. Who gave you this money?

Lender: Someone named Raman had come to meet me yesterday and he asked about the balance amount you were supposed to pay back. On sharing the details, he went to the nearby ATM and gave back the money by saying that Subhash has given the same.

Subhash: Ok, got it. Thanks, and bye.

Subhash was completely at a loss for words. Tears started rolling down his cheeks and he kept on sobbing for another 15 minutes. He just could not raise his head, unable to face Raman out of utter shame and disgrace. Raman read the situation quite well as the voice of the lender was quite audible to him.

Taking control of the situation, Raman gave a tight cozy hug to Subhash and tried to console him. Subhash unable to take any further embarrassment, just started speaking out feebly.

Subhash: I am sorry my friend. I was angry at you because you did not help me earlier when I needed the money direly. I should have been more considerate as you did not have money then. I misunderstood you badly, please excuse me.

Raman: It is ok Subhash. If I were in your place, I would have reacted in the same manner. Now, come on. Cheer up. You already have helped me on multiple occasions. I owe my stability in the job in this establishment and the city to you. So, whatever I did was just out of pure love and affection. And by the way, I am not going to leave that 30% amount. You will have to return me in the next

6 months or else I will not leave you. Maybe I would hire a dreaded criminal to get the money back from you in case you fail in doing so.

Subhash started laughing aloud on hearing how Raman had put the last punch of recruiting feared criminals in the end. Raman too smiled heartily as he has got his true friend back. Finally, genuine friendship won.

!!

Bonding

Anshika had just joined the premium college and was allotted a room in the hostel that she needed to share with one of her classmates. The space was clean but small, with barely enough area for two beds, a cupboard, and a pair of study tables. She was happy as her fellow mate would be joining a week later; thus, she had the luxury of staying in the room all alone. She preferred isolation and for her "**me time**" was of utmost priority.

In the evening, the seniors at the hostel invited all the freshers for a welcome party in the lounge area. This was a tradition in the shelter where everyone (both juniors and seniors) would get a chance to interact with each other and spend some casual fun moments together. A few cultural programs were scheduled and a disco jockey was arranged who would hit the floor later in the night with some foot-stomping music. The entire 1st-year batch was excited and eagerly waited for the sun to set as soon as possible.

In line with their expectation, the event turned out to be bombastic. There were songs, dances, and games that kept them engrossed & entertained throughout the night. Anshika, despite being an introvert enjoyed the get-together thoroughly. The next day she woke a bit late but had to finish all her chores quickly. She hated being late and especially on her first day in college. In hurry, she just forgot to take her purse. At lunchtime, she was too famished but could not go back to the hostel to collect it. It was prohibited by the warden to enter the same during college hours. She just walked towards the canteen and sat in a corner.

While she was completely captivated by her thoughts, an anonymous voice from behind startled her to the core.

Unknown: Hey, why do you look so confused?

Anshika: Excuse me, do I know you?

Unknown: My name is Vikrant and I am your batch mate.

Anshika: Ok, but I am not in the right frame of mind now to converse with you (Saying this she turned and started looking at the other side).

Vikrant strolled towards the canteen and bought a couple of sandwiches. He offered it to Anshika who refused it outrightly. From within she was cursing herself for declining it but that is how she was, sober and reserved. Despite her behaving a bit rudely, Vikrant dared to ask her again.

Vikrant: Madam, I do not like to eat alone. In my house, I always used to dine with my mom or my sister.

Anshika:(getting irritated) I am neither your mummy nor your sibling.

Vikrant: So, what? My mother has always taught me to share food with my friends.

This point hit a chord with the lady. She reminisced about the days at her home when her mother used to pamper her by making dishes of her choice regularly. She would give her a variety of foods in her tiffin asking her to share it with her pals. She turned towards Vikrant and took the sandwich from him. (God, she was dying of hunger)

Anshika: Thanks (saying this she took a bite of the food).

Vikrant: Mention not.

From thereon, both Anshika and Vikrant became good friends.

A week passed by and on the eighth day, the other girl arrived in her hostel room. Their first meeting was quite horrible and they almost had a fistfight. It so happened that the new girl, Reema put the entire luggage on the bed that belonged to Anshika. This made Anshika quite furious as she was finicky about cleanliness. She blasted on Reema which created a tense environment. Reema too was stubborn by nature and reverted harshly. Luckily the warden arrived at the spot while she was on her routine inspection. If the custodian did not intervene and interrupted in between, things could have taken an ugly turn.

For the next few weeks, there remained a cold war between the two girls. They would bitch about each other in front of their common friends. These pals would add salt & pepper to the conversations and do backbiting in front of both the lassies. This further deteriorated the already complex and strained relationship between both roommates. They would hardly talk with each other while in their hostel shelter. The only thing similar between both was Vikrant who was a dear friend to both. He was one such generous person who tried his best to improve the rapport between them. Unfortunately, even after numerous efforts, he too lost hope in creating a harmonious relationship between the two.

But destiny has its path and nobody is bigger than the circumstances created by some invisible energy. It so happened that one-night Reema fell ill. She got a high fever and was shivering out of the cold around 1 am in the mid of the night. While Anshika was busy doing her late-night study, she saw this and went near her bed. On checking her forehead, she got scared as it was burning hot. Immediately, she brought a thermometer to check the temperature. As expected, it showed 104 degrees Celsius. Anshika managed to get cold water and a cotton wrap which she applied continuously for 3-4 hours to lower her body hotness. Slowly and gradually, her body's heat dropped down. She remained awake all night to keep a check on her roommate. In the early morning, she informed the warden who arranged for a visit to a nearby general physician.

With this instance, the relationship between both girls took a U-turn. Reema thanked Anshika profusely for the selfless affection that she showed towards her. While Anshika remained neutral saying that she would have done this for anyone in distress. But Reema was now more thoughtful while speaking to her newly found friend. She has turned sweet and would take care of every little need of her roommate. Anshika too started responding to the love and attention that she was getting from Reema. Soon their relationship turned into a friendship wherein both spent maximum free time with each other. Be it the canteen or college campus or outings, both would be always seen together.

The strong bond between both friends got into the evil eyes of many of the classmates who envied the closeness they shared. A few would badmouth Reema in front of Anshika and some would criticize Anshika while discussing with Reema. But this never impacted their friendship as they would laugh out loud in the evening when alone in the hostel. They were sorted and understood the dirty politics of the people surrounding them.

Many tried to break their friendship or become a part of their group but no one succeeded. There was one girl named Medha who made an extra effort to join the duo. She would bring tasty home cooked from her house as she was a local girl from the same city. Both Anshika and Reema would relish the delicious dishes that Medha carried regularly for them. She would often gift them with a small modern electronic gadget for use or some kind of beautiful artificial jewelry to wear. She also won their heart when she took extra pain to make their respective birthdays special by arranging surprise get-togethers on the day. But there was something fishy about her as frequently a boy used to visit the campus to see her. They would chat for hours but whenever Anshika or Reema tried to ask about the mystery boy, she would divert the topic. Finally, the duo lost patience, and they confronted Megha one day.

Anshika: Hey, Medha why don't you ever disclose the detail of the person who comes to see you on and often?

Medha: I am not hiding anything from you (surprise and anger in her tone). He is my cousin brother; Rocky whose engineering college is very near to our campus. He just comes to chit-chat with me as we had spent quite a good time together in our childhood. He is quite attached to me, you know, as we are the almost same age.

Reema: Sorry, buddy. We misunderstood as we thought him to be your boyfriend. (There was regret in her voice)

Medha started laughing uncontrollably for a minute as if someone had cracked a joke in front of her.

Medha: No worries, tomorrow I would introduce him to you two. Hope that will clear all the air surrounding this secret guy.

They both smiled at seeing Medha being cheeky while saying the same. The next evening while Anshika and Seema were taking a walk on the campus, they saw Medha interacting with the same boy at a distance. Medha saw them and waved with a sign to join them. Seema was a bit reluctant but then Anshika insisted she meets them. The moment they reached the spot, Medha excitedly introduced her brother to them.

Medha: Anshika/Seema, meet my lovely brother Rocky. And Rocky, meet my two friends Seema and Anshika.

They all said 'Hello' to each other. Post that there was an awkward silence for a minute. Breaking the ice, Medha once again meddled to make the situation light and hearty.

Medha: Rocky, you shameless chap. Don't you see we three girls are waiting for you to ask us for a small treat?

Rocky: Oh, yes. Please all of you, let us have something.

Anshika: No, it is ok. We just had our evening snacks.

Seema: Ya, she is right. We are full to our throats.

Rocky: Ok, in that case, let us have a cup of coffee. A new coffee shop just got opened a week back. The reviews and feedbacks are excellent. I insist, that you all join me.

Medha: Come on, girls, coffee will be harmless and light for your stomach.

They could not say 'No' anymore and thus left for the place. Now, this became a very habitual activity. Every other day, all four would try some or other food in the nearby restaurants and cafés'. Most of the time, it would be Rocky who used to settle the bill (Despite Seema and Anshika insisting to pay the invoices). Even Medha would always prefer his brother to clear the cost of any sort of purchase and restrict her friends from paying for them. One fine day Rocky brought an expensive dress for both Anshika and Seema. They were not ready to take it but then once again Rocky stressed and convinced them to accept it. Both were a bit jumbled about the favour that the siblings were doing for them but then kept quiet as who does not like pampering?

One day Rocky out of blue invited Anshika and Seema for a lunch at his home. Though it sounded strange to them, Medha assured them that it was just that his brother wants their friends to meet his parents. Hearing this, both felt certain and relaxed. Rocky had come to pick them up from their hostel in an old car. That was a luxury for them as never before had they been given such a free ride in the city. They travelled for almost an hour in the vehicle, post which they reached the outskirt of the town. The vehicle stopped in front of an old building. Rocky parked the car and like a true gentleman opened the door for the ladies sitting inside. He then walked towards a narrow lane situated beside the torn ancient structure, and with sign language asked the girls to follow him. The road ahead was dingy, rather dark, and depressing. It was 1 pm noon but it appeared as if the sun is almost ready to set. The houses were so close to each other leaving no space for breathing. In such a small area, there were hundreds of houses. The ambiance of the place was not what they had expected, rather it was a locality full of filth and garbage surrounding it. Finally, they reached a house that was poorly maintained, with paint peeling off the walls. Rocky asked them to get into the house. The interior was shabbier with no ventilation and lighting inside the room. It was a bit creepy and Seema finally questioned Rocky;

Seema: Is this truly your house? Where are Uncle and Aunty?

Rocky: Yes, I was born here and have spent my childhood in the locality. Mom and Dad have gone to the temple. They may arrive at any moment, so please sit and make yourselves comfortable. I will be back some time.

Seema looked towards Anshika who looked tensed and worried. Seema too bit her lips in nervousness. Medha grasped the situation and tried to calm down the girls.

Medha: Rocky was born into a very poor family but now once he completes college, things would change for him and his family. He would bag a good job as he is studious in his studies.

Anshika: That we understood but Medha this place looks very different, not quite normal.

Medha: Everything is ok my friend. Anyways, we will leave sometime just after having lunch. Let Rocky parent's come. Meanwhile, I would go and get a cup of tea for both of you.

Anshika: OK

The moment Medha left for the kitchen, Anshika and Seema gave each other a suspicious look. With a whispering voice, Anshika conversed with Seema.

Anshika: Seema, something is not right. If Rocky is that poor, how could he afford frequent lunches and gifts for us?

Seema: I know, even I have the same feeling. Just look around at the posters of naked girls pasted on the wall.

Anshika: Yes, and while we were coming, I saw a few women who seemed like prostitutes. I think we are in the red-light area.

Seema: What are you saying? Why didn't you tell this me earlier?

Anshika: I wanted to say but was dead scared to utter a single word. I do not know why Rocky and Medha had invited us to such a horrible place.

Seema: Idiot. Are you a dumb person? Don't you understand they can push us into forced flesh trade? Or probably they can mix intoxicating material in food or drink served to us and then can take some objectionable pictures of us. In the future, they could blackmail us through them. Let us move out of the house. Hurry up, Anshika.

Without looking back, they walked as fast as possible. At one point they were running as if it were a matter of life and death. They did not stop till they reached a safe place near the main road. From there they took an auto and reached the hostel. What an escape it was! They took a sigh of relief and thanked their stars for getting respite from big trouble. They deleted Medha's number from their mobile and pledged not to ever talk to her again.

With this episode, the bond between the friends grew stronger. It was like two bodies and one soul, inseparable.

Time flies very fast and two years passed in the blink of an eye. There was not an iota of change in the friendship of the two pals but circumstances had altered. In the third and final year, Anshika was in love with Vikrant (the same boy mentioned at the beginning of the story) who through his sweet words won the heart of the lady. Seema was not at all happy with the relationship. Firstly, she felt dejected as Anshika now did not have enough time for her. Secondly, she did not find Vikrant to be a genuine guy. She would always try to convince Anshika to break her connection with Vikrant. But you know, love is blind. Anshika would ignore her warnings. One day Seema found Vikrant speaking with a girl on the phone which increased her doubt regarding his faithfulness towards Anshika. It was as if he was talking to his lady love in a very cozy tone. It unsettled her for a minute but then she straightaway went to Anshika to inform her about the incident.

Seema: Buddy, I am sure Vikrant is trying to manipulate you. I found him speaking to a girl on phone and the conversation was quite lovey-dovey as if she was her girlfriend.

Anshika: No way, you are such an insecure person. Why do you always want to create misunderstandings between us? But once and for all, I would clear your doubts. Come with me.

Saying this Anshika almost dragged Seema to the place where Vikrant was having his chat with the unknown person. Seeing them together, Vikrant got a bit startled.

Vikrant: Ladies, what are you up to? I mean two Goddesses together at the same time. It's quite an honor for me.

Anshika: Give me your phone and unlock it (There was anger in her voice).

Vikrant: But why? What is the matter?

Anshika: Do you love me?

Vikrant: Obviously yes, but that is not the answer to my question.

Anshika: Give me your phone Vikrant (She was getting quite impatient).

Vikrant: ok, take it.

Saying this he handed over the phone to Anshika. She wanted to see the last dialed number. Her heart sank on seeing the name of the person to whom Vikrant had called last. It was mentioned as 'Love'.

Anshika: Who is this '**Love**' Vikrant?

Vikrant: You are conducting an illegal act. This is called an infringement of privacy which is a non-bailable warrant case if found guilty (He was as jovial as always).

Anshika: Shut up. How can you do such a cheap joke in such a situation? Tell me who is this '**Love**'?

Vikrant: Ok, better you call on this number and find it out yourself.

Anshika immediately started dialling the number. Knowingly she kept the phone on speaker mode so that everyone can hear the conversation. From the other side, an adult voice replied, 'Yes, Son. What happened? I informed you, not to call me for another 1 hour as I am in my gymnasium class'. Vikrant immediately answered, 'Sorry Mama, take care. Will speak to you later.'

There was a pin-drop silence for a minute. Anshika finally broke the quietness.

Anshika: Seema, are you convinced now, or do you still doubt Vikrant?

Vikrant: What doubt are you talking about?

Anshika: Nothing. It is just girl's talk.

Seema stood there motionless like a statue. It seemed as if she had been stupefied. She was not able to look into Anshika's eyes out of guilt and shame.

They all dispersed but still, Seema was not satisfied with the outcome. Even though she got embarrassed, she had a strong feeling that Vikrant was hiding something.

Seema wanted to save her dear friend from the evil eyes of Vikrant. She got cautious and started investigating Vikrant's activities. For a week, she acted like a detective following him everywhere. Once while scrutinizing his deeds, she overheard him speaking to someone to meet in a nearby garden at 4 pm today. She followed her instinct and planned to go to the same location to see what Vikrant was up to. At that exact time, she reached the spot and hid behind a tree. The orchard was almost empty. At 10 past 4, a beautiful girl walked in and sat on a bench nearby. By 4:20 PM, Vikrant too arrived and paced toward the site where the girl was sitting. On reaching, Vikrant hugged her and gave her a peck on the cheek. The girl smiled and blushed as if she is meeting the man of her life. Seema was ready with the mobile camera and kept on clicking photos. Both kept conversing with each other for an hour. Seema was getting bored as she wanted to see some kind of action that can concretely prove her point to Anshika. At a point when she was losing hope, suddenly Vikrant pulled the girl towards him and then smooched her passionately. This continued for two long minutes which she captured on her mobile camera. Not interested any further, she just ran out of the park and left for the hostel.

There was a sense of accomplishment in her mind but her heart just sank at the very thought of how Anshika would react to this. But this was something which she had done for her friend. The real face of Vikrant needed to come out clearly in front of her. The moment she reached her room, she found Anshika reading a book in a very relaxed manner. Without wasting any time, she showed all the pictures and videos of the incident. Anshika was heartbroken and she cried the entire night. Her eyes were swollen and her face has turned pale. It was hard for Seema to see this but she knew the matter is not yet over. Anshika owed an explanation from Vikrant. He was completely exposed now.

For two days Anshika remained indoors, she was shattered and devastated. Vikrant kept calling her but she did not pick up his call. The only relief for her was the presence of her evergreen friend Seema. She had stayed back at the hostel taking care of Anshika. The only solution to bringing this story to an end was a heart-to-heart discussion with Vikrant. Thus, Seema called Vikrant to meet Anshika at the hostel. She told him that Anshika is not keeping well for the last two days. On hearing this, Vikrant immediately landed at the gate of the girl's hostel. Seema somehow encouraged Anshika to meet him and close this chapter permanently.

Anshika found Vikrant waiting for her impatiently. She walked towards him and with a forced smile on her face, started speaking to Vikrant.

Anshika: Hi, Vikrant.

Vikrant: Hello, Anshika. Why did you not inform me that you were ill? I would have taken you to the doctor. You also did not pick up my innumerable calls (He almost yelled at Anshika).

Anshika: It is ok. My condition was not that so bad and you know I am a strong girl. I did not pick up your call as I did not want to. By the way, just check your phone. I have sent some pictures and videos which you would find very interesting.

Vikrant: Certainly.

Saying this Vikrant started checking all the images sent to her. He was shell-shocked. His dubious character has been completely bared by substantial proof. He was just not able to utter a single word.

Anshika: You know Vikrant, trust is the backbone of any relationship. You have broken it brutally. I do not want to defame you by sharing these with anyone. I just want to say that get the hell out of here and never show me your face again.

Saying this she deleted everything on the mobile in front of Vikrant and left the spot hurriedly.

Back into the hostel room, she again wept profusely. Luckily, she had the shoulder of her best buddy, Seema, to console and motivate her.

This is what true bonding is all about. You always walk the extra mile to protect and save people whom you love and adore.

Partnership

Amit and Ravi were the talks of the small town, Patratu in the Ramgarh district of the state Jharkhand. The teachers at Kendriya Vidyalaya had high hopes for both in the 12th board exam. Kendriya Vidyalaya is a system of central government schools in India that are instituted under the aegis of the Ministry of Education, Government of India. While Amit was in Commerce stream, Ravi was enrolled in science. Both shared a great friendship since their early childhood. Amit's dad was posted as an officer in the electrical department of Patratu Thermal Power Station and Ravi's father was a worker in the mechanical division of the same organization. The difference in the strata of their respective guardian never came in the camaraderie they had between them.

They both had similar kinds of passion when it came to academics. They always craved learning and knowledge. While Ravi was the school captain, Amit was designated with the responsibility of sports captain. Both were all-rounders, be it a debate, quiz, skit, song, or game, the duo excelled in everything. The juniors followed their every activity like a swarm of bees.

Like the belief that everyone had about them, they topped the board exam with flying marks. Their score was the highest in the entire state in the respective course they had opted for. Through his hard work, Ravi qualified for the Indian Institute of Technology, Kharagpur for Engineering. Similarly, Amit cracked 5 years of integrated bachelor's and Master's in Business administration from the Indian Institute of Management, Indore.

Just after one month of the result declaration, they moved to a different location for further studies. Yet they remain connected on regular basis. They would discuss their vision and dreams for themselves. One thing common among them was that they both wanted to take a step toward entrepreneurship. They knew that it would be a different ballgame to make their parents come to terms with their aspirations but eventually, they planned of realizing their ultimate mission.

Time flies very fast, Ravi completed his four-year Engineering program and got recruited as a Software Engineer in a top inventory and accounting ERP company. In the 1st year, he was part of the back-end, front-end, and database management team which were involved in the core development of the product. In the second year, he was transferred to the Android development division where he learned the process of developing specific applications for explicit use.

On the other hand, Amit joined as the Marketing lead in a top FMCG company after completing his MBA from the reputed institute. He closely worked with the product and sales team to bring in the best ways of promoting and selling the brand. Digital marketing, vendor management, and enhancing the organization's visibility in the country was his key job.

For a brief time, both friends lost contact with each other. They both got so busy in their job that they missed the frequent discussions they used to have in the past. But the fire of doing their own business remained alive in their heart. It so happened that Amit had come to Delhi from Mumbai to attend the company's annual conference. He knew that Ravi was based out of Delhi but he had lost his contact details. Thus, he activated all his contacts to get his mobile number. After a lot of endeavors, he got it from one of his common friends. Thus, on reaching Delhi, he called up Ravi:

Amit: Idiot, where are you?

Ravi: (Immediately recognized his voice) Bro, at the office. Are you by any chance in town?

Amit: Bingo. So, get ready for a grandiloquent evening. Let us meet up at a pub in Connaught Place.

Ravi: Done. I will be there by 8 pm.

Amit: Great (Saying this he hung up the phone)

Throughout the day, Ravi remained excited as after a long time he was going to meet his childhood friend. At 7 pm sharp, he left for the location decided earlier. The music inside the pub was loud but full of fun. Amit too arrived at the place on time. There was so much excitement in the air and the moment they met, both hugged each other tightly as if they are not going to meet again.

Amit: I am very hungry buddy. Let us order something.

Ravi: Are you joking? Run through the 'Drinks' menu immediately. I cannot allow you to have food, before the alcohol.

Amit: Oh! I too had the same intention. Food takes time, that is why I wanted to order it prior. Anyways, what would you like to have?

Ravi: Bro, let us have single malt. See for many days I did not get a chance to go to any bar. Good that you have come, I don't want to remain in my senses today.

Amit: Hero, don't worry. We have the entire night with us.

Saying this they ordered the best single malt whiskey. With every peg, they both started opening with each other.

Ravi: Bro, I am not happy with my job. My ultimate desire was to run my own business where I would have products that had been exclusively developed by me. I wanted to create something that would have brought a difference in the lives of millions of people around. I wanted to be an enabler in giving employment to people. But, alas, I have failed myself. See, day, and night I am working for a company and earning revenue for them.

Amit: Same here dear. I too inclined to drive my organization with a crore of the turnover year after year. I wanted to live a life where I am the owner of my destiny. But see what am I up to? I am living the dreams of my institution, running after targets, and accomplishing their vision. I have lost enthusiasm in my life.

Ravi: Amit, we had decided to open our establishment together. I have an idea which if you say we can try to implement in the market. The blueprint of the same is ready. To be true, the product is 50% complete (He then explained his concept to Amit in brief). I will be the Chief

Technical Officer of the company and you the Chief Marketing Officer. Can't we work together to fulfill our lost dream?

Amit: Ravi I trust in your instincts and I am excited about the project. The plan looks concrete but what about the fund?

Ravi: Do not worry. I had saved every penny while working. I knew that someday you would join me.

Amit: I too have some fixed deposits that I would break to start this journey.

Ravi: Then let us go for it.

They stayed at the bar till the last person had left the zone.

Early in the morning, both typed a resignation mail to their respective bosses. They had planned that they would initially work from home and then as the venture takes up, they would rent out an office. After just one month, Amit permanently shifted to Delhi to be with his partner cum friend. He knew that Ravi would require his emotional and moral support.

The product was a GST-based (Goods & Service Taxes) software that would help businessmen in filing their taxes in a very convenient way. Their prime purpose was to target the big market size of micro small medium enterprises. There were a few competitors in the market but they would prove ineffective with the introduction of the advanced product whose sketch was ready with Ravi. He started working on it with pure devotion and effort. Within two months, the hard work has shown results as the same was prepared for the first presentation of their lives. Amit, being in marketing, was a bit outspoken. He took the lead while influencing the client, while Ravi showcased the product with complete confidence. The name that they registered for their organization was "RAAM Solutions Private Limited"(RA from Ravi and AM from Amit).

They started pitching in the product to consumers. One of the customers was happy with the demo and this was a watershed moment for them. The first deal for the company got cracked. They celebrated with a simple cake cutting back at their home. Slowly and gradually, they started conquering the market. By the sixth month, they had earned enough to rent out an office. They needed support guys for implementation and taking care of the existing client base. Thus, they added 2-3 people to the team for the same. By end of 1st year, they had acquired around 300 customers with a very good margin. The profit that they were getting from the GST software sale was around 80%. The employee count had increased from 3 to 21 people. After cutting all the operating expenses and other costs, they were earning decent money. Now they also started targeting enterprise customers.

The only and biggest challenge with them was an investment. Both Ravi and Amit knew that with the expertise they both were carrying; they would be easily able to attract investors. The product was robust and they were getting excellent feedback from the customer end. The hurdle was Ravi himself, as he did not want the intervention of any third person in the business as of now. The investor would try to meddle in the affairs of the company if they do not get the returns that they had been promised while getting the deal.

This would create unnecessary pressure on the system. While Amit had a different belief altogether. According to him, they should invite venture capitalists into their business. It's not only finances that they would bring to the occupation, they would also add expertise in operations, sales, and marketing. To scale up the revenue of the organization, they needed money for marketing and penetration of the product. Generally, these investors are already the owner of some kind of trade, thus they are accustomed to the ups and downs of the establishment. Nevertheless, they could be good guides and mentors.

Both had strong logic behind their point and thus they were not able to come to a common platform. This created unwanted strain in their relationship. This also started impacting the performance of the institution. Now, they were not working as a team. Small issues that could have been sorted through discussion started getting stuck. The lack of communication between them led to various failures of end-customer deals. A time came when both stopped talking to each other. The entire employee ecosystem felt the differences that had cropped up in the organization. The office where the environment was always filled with fun had now turned sober. People started leaving the company as sales dropped. The financial health of the establishment started deteriorating. Finally, one day Ravi decided to have a man-to-man discussion with Amit.

Ravi: Amit, what is your final decision?

Amit: I shared this with you earlier also. We need investors by hook or crook. I cannot wait for an indefinite period to see the institution grow. It is now or never.

Ravi: But Amit, can't we be more patient? I mean just for another 2-3 years. I am sure by then we would grow as the acceptability and demand of the product are growing.

Amit: Ravi, I cannot wait for even a single month.

Ravi: In that case, we cannot work together Amit. You need to decide and let me know your final decision whenever you feel like it.

Amit: Do not worry Ravi. I would share the same by tomorrow itself. I am also fed up with the uncertainty surrounding us. This cold war amongst us will not do any good to us.

Amit left the space immediately as he needed some **'me'** time for himself. The next day Ravi had not come to the office. Amit had made up his mind and thus called Ravi to inform him of the decision that he has taken.

Amit: Hi Ravi, where are you today?

Ravi: Got some work at the bank. Will call you back in some time (saying this he disconnected the call).

Amit wanted to clear the air of confusion as soon as possible. Today he will finally end their partnership. He thought of calling him back after an hour to convey his decision of quitting the conglomerate. While he was in his deep thoughts, the sound of a call from his mobile startled him. He picked it up as it was a call back from Ravi. He started speaking:

Amit: What happened? Are you free now? Can we talk?

From the other side, an unknown voice spoke in a very disturbed tone. "Sir, your friend has met an accident. We are taking him to SRL Hospital based at Arthur Road. I got your number from the last dialled list of your friend. Probably the last call he made was to you. Please come as fast as possible."

Amit frantically ran outside the office towards his parked car. He drove with the ultimate speed and reached the hospital in just half an hour. At the reception counter, he came to know that Ravi had been taken to the operation theatre as surgery was required due to multiple fractures in both his legs. The nurse walked toward him to take the necessary signature required as a formality (as there was no one else who could have done that at this point). Amit informed Ravi's parents about the mishap who were based out of a far-off city, Kolkata, almost 1500 km away from Delhi. It was 10 PM now and the guardians of his friend would be able to reach latest by tomorrow morning. The operation went on for 2 complete hours and Amit remained awake the whole night waiting for his friend to regain consciousness.

The next morning at around 9 am, Ravi opened his eyes. His parents had arrived by then from the first flight available for the city. He was in acute agony as the painkillers given to him had stopped showing its result after 10 hours. He saw his mom and dad sitting beside him. For a minute he was not able to understand what has happened. Amit took control of the situation and explained the entire episode to Ravi. He asked Ravi to take a rest.

For 15 days, Ravi remained hospitalized and every day Amit would come to see him after office hours. On the last day, when Ravi was supposed to be discharged, Amit brought flowers for him.

Amit: Buddy, now you are ok. Just that you need one more month to stay at home to recuperate from your discomfort.

Ravi: Thanks for being with me in my tough time Amit. Pal, what have you decided about our partnership?

Amit: Nothing. Was there any difference between us? (Amit said as if there was no disagreement between them). I am in sync with you, we need to give time to our company for another 2-3 years. Probably, after that, we could invite investors if we fail.

Ravi for a second was dumbstruck. He just could not believe his ears. Tears started rolling down his cheeks (Amit had forgone his vision for the sake of their friendship as he knew that this is not the right time to remain stubborn. His companion needed his support badly).

Amit: You are a drama king. Stop showing your emotional side to me. Probably I would also start crying.

Both the friends gave a high-five and smiled at each other. Amit had done a sacrifice as his friend needed him at this crucial juncture. He could not leave his buddy to fend for himself in this difficult time. Finally, the partnership remained intact but the most important thing was that their friendship remained unscathed and untouched.

Revenge

Shibani and Anwesh had started their career as sales executives in the company together. They both were hard-working, efficient, and sincere personnel in their job. The owner of the organization Mr. Mehta realized this in the very first month of their joining his establishment. He believed in giving chances to youngsters who are eager to prove their worth in the highly fierce corporate world. True to his principles, Mr. Mehta started grooming them for future leadership roles. Both were aligned with the best managers in the institution. Very soon the result started showing, the duo began giving an excellent performance in their respective area. Thus, the management took a step to give more responsibility to these bright workers. In just 7 years, from sales executive, they had been accorded the profile of Zonal managers. Anwesh was the Zonal Sales head for North & East whereas Shibani led the South & West regions.

With time the friendship between the two colleagues had grown. They would support each other in every forum. Their unity had been instrumental in getting major approvals of various beneficial activities for the team and the partner network in record time. Thus, they became quite popular in both crucial ecosystems. Together they had taken the institution to the level where it reached the Top 5 establishments of the industry in the country. Due to this, Mr. Mehta allowed them to take calls on major decisions of the organization. The good thing was that on almost all the issues, their viewpoints matched, thus there was no scope for clashes between them. They reported to the National Head whose role and importance in the company were dubious. He played a dummy role as he did what was suggested by the ZM. The Zonal heads would finally push him to take verdicts as per their wishes. The other cross-functional departments, like the customer service or training department, or HR divisions, would take calls as per the recommendation of the Zonal heads. But there was a reason for their supremacy. It was always backed by power-packed strong productivity, performance, profitability, output, and growth that were beneficial for the institution. Mr. Mehta had high regard for this and he had complete faith in his favorite lieutenants.

Probably it was this authority of the Zonal Managers which was not liked by many. The biggest opposer of their acts was their reporting manager, that is the National Head. He always felt that his notions were negated by both his immediate subordinates. Somewhere in his mind, he had a view that the Zonal Managers could pose a threat to his position in the company. Other senior leaders too never liked the due importance that was always given to the duo. But who cared, Anwesh and Shibani were the unannounced kings of the organization. Because of this, a game of planning and plotting started being hatched against them.

The biggest challenge in the professional arena is overcoming insecurity. People use all kinds of manipulations to safeguard their position in the corporate world. Both Anwesh and Shibani, the two protagonists of this story became the prey of jealousy, anxiety, and distrust.

The best way to break the unity was to create friction among them. So, one fine day the National Head called Anwesh in his cabin in the context of some kind of business discussion of his region.

National Head: Anwesh, your region is doing quite well. I am happy with how you guide your team and partners in achieving the organizational goal. Good job buddy.

Anwesh: Thank you sir for making my day. (He replied enthusiastically).

The National Head continued;

National Head: I see a huge potential in you. You could be the next National Head of this organization.

Anwesh: Are you kidding sir? I mean I just have 10 years of work exposure. I would require another 4-5 years to even think about the profile suggested by you.

National Head: Anwesh, my experience says that you are ready for the next big role. I might be retiring in a year or two and would join the organization's board as an executive member. My part would be more of a consultative and someone capable like you would lead the sales nationally.

Anwesh: Thank you for the consideration, sir.

National Head: It is my pleasure. Do not discuss this with anyone as I need to suggest the same to Mr. Mehta once you are all right with it.

Anwesh: Ok sir, please go ahead.

This was the first time that Anwesh did not share the discussion he had with the National Head with Shibani. He was in a confused state of mind but was happy that his proficiencies are being noticed by the senior management. Anwesh was not able to gauge the evil intentions behind it. The National Head on the other hand had played his game well. He never wanted to leave the company for another 10 years and was keen on continuing the current role that he was playing in the establishment. He did this just to create a bridge between the two friends.

The next day, the National Head went to Mr. Mehta to discuss some important issues.

Mr. Mehta: Why are our revenues not at par with our competitors? We were well ahead of them last year but currently, we are lagging behind them by a good margin.

National Head: Sir, I am trying my best to minimize the gap but facing a few challenges.

Mr. Mehta: What are those? (there was a sense of concern in his voice)

National Head: Most of them can be taken care of but the acute challenge lies in the way Anwesh is behaving. The revenue could have quadrupled as the market of North & East has grown for every other company with a similar product line as ours. But our Zonal Head Anwesh on the other hand is busy, aspiring to become the National Sales Head of the company. His thought process seemed very disoriented and unsettled. Yesterday I had a brief discussion regarding the same and he expressed his desire for the designation. He also threatened to leave the organization in case his demand is not fulfilled. I tried to reason that it is too early for him to lead the country but he remained adamant on his claim (The National Head very cleverly manipulated the discussions that were straightaway targeted against Anwesh).

Mr. Mehta: This cannot be true. I mean, I think he has been influenced by someone. He is doing quite well but I strongly feel that at this point he is not ready for the big task and accountabilities. I could not digest that he had requested for the growth. Anwesh is a nice guy who has been faithful to the organization in its worst periods. He will never leave us. Let me have a word with him.

Saying this, Mr. Mehta left the meeting abruptly. He was saddened and anxious by the current situation. Both Anwesh and Shibani were his weakness as he was the one who had been keenly observing and pushing their growth in the establishment. He knew them personally, had been to their houses, and celebrated all their achievements together. Mr. Mehta could not sleep the whole night. The next morning, he called Anwesh to his cabin. Anwesh was alarmed as one on one meeting with the owner was never considered normal in the institution. He knew that Mr. Mehta used to call them only when he wanted to discuss some crucial points. He cautiously entered the room.

Anwesh: Good morning, sir.

Mr. Mehta: Good morning, Anwesh. How are you doing my friend?

Anwesh: I am ok sir. Hope I have not done any mistakes.

Mr. Mehta: (smiling) What made you think so?

Anwesh: Sir, we all know that your cabin is a 'Hot room.' Normal discussions are done in the conference halls but if the person is called in here, then the matter is of utmost importance.

Mr. Mehta could not stop smiling but then he knew the exact purpose. He started speaking again;

Mr. Mehta: Anwesh, do you desire to become the National Head?

Anwesh: Why not sir? If given the opportunity, I would grab it with both my hands.

Mr. Mehta: Hmm. Ok, you can leave. Let me think about it.

Anwesh was a bit surprised and disappointed. Astonished, because Mr. Mehta did not continue the discussion and asked him to leave in just a minute. Disappointed because he was not able to understand what transpired behind his back. He could only assume that the National Head had probably recommended his name to Mr. Mehta for the post. But the strange behavior of the owner left him in a confused and depressed state of mind.

The National Head knew that this matter would not remain confined to just three of them. He was aware that Mr. Mehta had a habit of sharing the challenges with Shibani. He was considered among the few with whom the owner used to confide all important issues. The owner discussed this scenario with him to take his opinion. Though nobody came to know the conversation between them, things had changed from thereon.

The relationship between Anwesh and Shibani had started deteriorating. Anwesh had to face the heat and anguish of his colleague cum friend, Shibani. He would often taunt and tease Anwesh for his ambition. The targets set by the National Head for the North & East region were unachievable. This was done in complete collaboration with Shibani. For a complete quarter, Anwesh could not do his numbers and thus missed getting the incentives. His viewpoints regarding business activity started getting ignored. It was as if his perspective is of no importance. The person who was always an award winner in almost every quarter for exceptional performance was side-lined unceremoniously. This went on for quite some time. Anwesh was at a loss for words. He just could not understand what was happening to him. He was under acute mental stress and depression. His good friend has turned into a foe for no fault of his. He had no shoulders left to cry upon. Anwesh tried connecting with Mr. Mehta many a time to highlight the same but his voice remains unheard.

Other department heads were also happy to see the loss of harmony among the Zonal heads. They would discuss the same in a whisper behind their back. But was it ok for the ecosystem? You would come to know in the second half of the story.

Frustrated by the indifferent approach of the senior management, Anwesh took the final step of leaving the establishment. Luckily, he got an opportunity as the National

Head of sales in a startup company. The last day for Anwesh at his office was quite emotional. His team from various parts had arrived at the office to bid farewell. They all were in tears as the association with him was for a substantial period. The partner network started pouring heartfelt wishes to their favorite ZM. There was lots of melodrama at the workplace and it seemed that each of them is undergoing the pain of some sort of personal loss. But some people were quite happy with the development. The National head and other senior leaders were glad as they have finally succeeded in secluding one of their competitors. Mr. Mehta had come to meet Anwesh at the final moments when he said all good things about him. He proposed that Anwesh returns to the institution whenever he feels like it. The doors would always remain open for him.

On the other hand, Anwesh had internally taken a pledge that he would never like to see the faces of people who had tried to ruin his career and peace of mind. He was particularly angry with Shibani and Mr. Mehta whom he had always considered a friend and mentor in his life. Deep inside, a fire was burning to take revenge on them. But for the time being, the upfront task was to settle down in his new organization. The startup was just 3 years old with a very similar product line to his previous company. The good part was that it was being funded by top venture capitalists. Thus, there was no dearth of investment. The second good aspect was the quality of the product. It was developed with the latest technology and per the demand of the customer. The owner of the institution gave Anwesh the full liberty to take decisions in product, sales, marketing, and customer service. Anwesh took the challenging role of developing the product, team, and partner network that can take the organization to next level. In just one year he had brought the institution to a breakeven point which was quite remarkable. From the 2nd year, the startup had turned into a profitable undertaking with 400% growth. The institution received the best upcoming MSME startup award from the Ministry of Industry. The interview with Anwesh got published in various newspapers and TV channels. Mr. Mehta and Shibani came to know about it. They called Anwesh to congratulate him.

On contrary, the organization of Mr. Mehta was in a bad state. After the exit of Anwesh, a new manager was appointed for the zone. He was not able to gel with the team and partners properly. The business started dipping. Many employees began leaving the establishment. There was complete chaos in the system. Partner complaints kept on piling up but there was no one in the organization to listen. Customers started churning but there was no one to solve their issues. Shibani himself was demotivated as he had lost his zeal after his friend cum colleague's departure. The condition of the National Head was worse and due to poor performance, he was asked to leave. Mr. Mehta many a time tried to retain Anwesh back in the system but every time he turned down the offer. Somewhere Mr. Mehta was fed up with the anarchy prevailing in the company and was planning to sell it off.

The new company where Anwesh had joined was growing like anything. From a 10-crore company annually, it had grown to 1000 crore in just 5 years. The owner of the organization wanted to expand. Thus, one day he called Anwesh for suggestions.

Owner: Anwesh, the investors have asked us to acquire our major competitor so that we get some kind of monopoly in the country. Who do you think would be our best catch? Do not worry about the investment, the financers would back us blindfolded. They are very happy with the way we have driven the company.

Anwesh: Sir, we have just 3 institutions that can be considered for this proposal. But if you trust me, the organization Mr. Mehta owns would be best suited. First, the partner network of the company is very strong. Thus, we can easily reap the benefit of that. Secondly, they have a quality customer base and this matches our culture. Thirdly, their market share is at a downfall making it a very lucrative option for us to buy.

Owner: Ok, let me check with the investors first. Remember, you will have the additional responsibility of leading it along with this establishment.

Anwesh: Do not worry sir, trust me, I will manage.

Anwesh believed in the theory "Forgive but never Forget". He had knowingly pitched Mr. Mehta's company as obtaining it would be a kind of achievement for him. He would be leading the organization that forced him to leave it. In the next few months, the owner of his current institution cracked the deal with Mr. Mehta's company in a ratio of 51%:49%. Mr. Mehta owned 49%, which meant he would not be dominant in the organization. The new owner with 51% after the merger immediately asked Anwesh to take over responsibility for taking strategic decisions there.

In the new setup, Mr. Mehta needs to take the approval of Anwesh for every major pronouncement. This was very humiliating as now he had to visit Anwesh's cabin to take his consent. The condition of Shibani was worse as he was now subordinate to Anwesh. It was very embarrassing for him as he was reporting to a person who was his colleague and friend in the past. He tried a lot to change the institution but nobody took him. The world is small and everybody knew how he with help of senior management had incorrectly removed an excellent employee like Anwesh from the system. Thus he lacked credibility in the market due to which nobody was ready to recruit him.

Anwesh had taken the sweet vengeance. He was not happy to see all this but yes he had a sense of satisfaction in his heart. He had taken revenge on people who had wronged him for his no mistake.

Promise

The campus interview had started creating a very sober and tense situation for all the students. The institute ranked in the top 10 as far as management schools in India were concerned. The top-notch organization used to storm this premier college for recruitment.

Riya, Sneha, Akansha, and Jolly were best of friends. They all were in the final year of their course and rigorously preparing for the entire employment process. The only exception was Jolly who wanted to be an entrepreneur. Her father owned two small cafes in Mumbai and thus she aspired to spread its branches across India. To prepare for the recruitment, the rest three would engage in group discussion and mock interviews amongst themselves. This was possible because they all stayed in the same hostel (None of them belonged to the city). That is why their bond grew special and stronger with a period. They stood with each other in thin and thick times.

On the very first week, when the companies had just started coming for selection, the three friends got enlisted for the finest jobs in reputed organizations. While Riya bagged a job in a renowned Banking establishment based out of America, Sneha got an offer from a prestigious Information technology company based in Dubai, whereas Akansha competed and got chosen for a prominent manufacturing institution in Chennai. The ladies were brimming with excitement and joyousness. The same evening they all planned for a get-together in a posh restaurant which they had always dreamt of going to. Jolly was unaffected by all these as she knew what she wanted to achieve in her life. But she was very happy for her friends. They declared it **"Accomplishment Day"** as today they have been able to realize the aspirations they always visualized for. They stayed back till late at night at the eatery and had complete fun. They promised each other that on this particular date i.e **19**[th] **August,** they would meet every year. They rather pledged that what come what may, they would gather on this day anyhow, irrespective of the situation or place they are in.

One year down the line, they all became busy in their job and occupation. As they were freshers, thus learning and adjusting to the current environment was of utmost priority. The good thing about them was their sincerity and quick learning capability. Despite their hectic schedule, all remembered the 19th of August and gathered at Bangalore on the 1st year of completion after their separation from the college. The star point was that within a year Jolly had opened three more stores, taking the count to five. They all assembled at her flagship coffee shop. The four friends had a gala time and they shared their experiences in their respective fields. Riya, Sneha, & Akansha were liking their job and did quite well in their respective sphere. Nothing had changed between them and the worthy aspect of this meeting was that the equation between them remained intact as before. The affection, bond, and love stayed the same as they used to be during their college time. Just one thing had altered, now they had enough money to order any kind of dish they wanted to relish from the menu.

They all were big foodies and bonded well at any gourmet. But here also they were at an advantage as the entire expenses were being borne by Jolly who did not allow anyone to spend a single penny at her outlet.

In the 2nd year, the circumstance became quite different. They all got too busy and were not able to come on the scheduled date. The pressure of the job and lack of time has taken away the charm of meeting old friends. The ambition of growing, leading, and succeeding has eventually faded the excitement they had in the 1st year of the get-together. Though they were in touch with each other through phone, chats, and various social media platforms, the enchantment of that physical contact has been lost with time. It was not that they do not want to meet, but their existing genuine engagements would always come in the way.

Twenty-Four years passed with a flick of an eye. By now Riya had become the Vice-President of her company, Sneha has attained the Chief Technology Officer profile and Akansha was the Group Plant Head of the organization. Jolly with her expertise has opened around 200 stores in Pan India and abroad which was a huge milestone in her business domain. On the personal front, except for Sneha, everybody else had married and had kids. Riya had two children, a boy, and a girl, whereas Jolly and Akansha had one girl child each. Sneha did not believe in the institution of marriage and thus lived a solitary life. The virtuous facet was that she never regretted the decision.

An age comes when you start reminiscing about the good old days. The four friends have achieved what they wanted to attain in their careers. Their kids were adults now and had chosen their respective professions as per their wishes. Thus, there was no liability in their lives. It ignited a will in the hearts of four friends to meet once again.

Jolly initiated the call two months before 19th August of the twenty-fifth year. They all spoke to each other and planned to meet on the same day once again. This time they had all the time on earth to spare for each other. Relieved from the major responsibility of enabling their kids to stand tall in their occupation and making them ready to take their decisions independently was a major achievement for them.

This time they wanted to celebrate it elaborately as it also was an occasion to rejoice in their long-standing friendship that has seen the test of times. They all were super thrilled and thus had made all flight tickets and various other arrangements in advance. The location was the same i.e., Bangalore at the same flagship coffee shop of Jolly. To make this trip remarkable, they had together planned a day visit to their old institute where this friendship had started.

Finally, D-day arrived and the three friends landed at the Bangalore Airport one by one. As the timings varied by just one or two hours, the three friends Sneha, Riya, and Akansha waited for else at the lounge. They all were so happy to see each other after a long time. It was as if they have got a new lease on life. All those evergreen memories of their college days started flashing before their eyes. There were a few wrinkles on their faces and bodies, and their expression showed tiredness after a long tiresome journey but their eyes twinkled like a star. On just seeing each other, they suddenly started feeling young, rejuvenated, and lively. The transformation was so natural, it seemed they had been never away from each other. All had lots of things to discuss, talk about, and convey. From the airport, they took a cab and shared their life stories on their way to the coffee shop. By evening around 8 pm, they had reached the grand outlet of Jolly.

The ladies were thrilled that they would be seeing their fourth pal, the entrepreneur in a moment. The instant they entered the cafe, a sweet girl escorted them to a reserved table.

Riya: Wow, now this is something Jolly could have only planned.

They all were curious as to how the girl recognized who they were. Thus, out of inquisitiveness, Sneha asked her;

Sneha: How do you know us and why did you escort us to a 'reserved' table?

Girl: Mam, your photo was shown to me by my boss. She had instructed me to take care of all your needs till the time she arrives.

Akansha: What do you mean by 'arrive'? Isn't she available today?

Girl: Mam, she had a very critical meeting with one of the investors who is going to finance a few more stores that we are planning to open abroad. She is in town but would reach a bit late. Make yourself comfortable and I would inform her about your advent.

Saying this the girl left after handing over the mocktail menu to the ladies.

Riya: Great. See we all remained an employee our whole lives. Jolly employs more than 3000 people. We run behind corporate clients and she deals with the venture capitalist.

Sneha: So who told you not to be an entrepreneur? It is not too late now. Go for it, madam.

The way Sneha spoke sarcastically, a smile flashed on the face of Riya and Akansha.

They all kept sharing and cherishing all the light moments non-stop. Meanwhile, the girl came to the table once again to take the order. They all requested Virgin Margarita with garlic bread as the starter. The topic of conversation kept on varying, sometimes it was about their personal lives, then suddenly they would start discussing their work, and at times they would also remember the good old college days. Thus there was no ending to their chats, they wanted to know everything about each other that has happened in their respective lives in the last 24 years.

It was 9:30 PM by now. There was no sign of Jolly yet. They at least wished to have dinner with her. Thus, losing out their patience, they called out to the girl.

Akansha: Dear, when will your mam come? Can you just call her and confirm? We do not want to disturb her as maybe she is in between some important deal.

Girl: Mam, I just spoke to her. It will take another two hours for her to come. Meanwhile, you can order dinner.

For the first time, since they had met, the three ladies felt a bit disappointed. They badly wanted to meet Jolly. They looked at each other with sad looks. But finally decided to have dinner as they were hungry. So, they ordered Pizzas & Pasta. In just 15 minutes everything was beautifully displayed at their table. They slowly ate the food with the hope of meeting their fourth friend thereafter. By 11 pm they were done with the feast and now finally the desserts were also served to them. This made the three friends a bit angry;

Riya: What is this? Doesn't Jolly know the importance of this meeting? Was this not on her priority list?

Sneha: It seems to me, that the business is far more important for her than her friends.

Akansha: We too were busy but took out time for this precious moment. This is not done. Let her come first, we would leave immediately the moment she arrives.

Riya: Yes, I will not wait for even a single second.

At 11:30 PM, a young girl walked in towards their seating. From a distance, she resembled almost like their friend Jolly. They were nearly sure that their old pal has finally arrived. But their excitement soon vanished the moment she came close to them. The girl who looked like their friend was too young. The lass wished everyone and just sat beside them (as if she is an old acquaintance with them).

Young Girl: Hi, my name is Avantika and I am the daughter of Jolly, your good old friend.

For a second the three friends got confused but then understood the whole situation.

Sneha: Ok, young lady, that is why your face reminds me of your mama.

Riya: Wow, your smile is very similar to Jolly's.

Akansha: But we all are very annoyed with her as she did not meet us at the stipulated time as promised. Now she has sent you to pacify us. So bad of her.

Avantika: No, no, she is not bad. She told me to take care of you three. My mother had shared the entire itinerary as to what your plans were. But she could not make it to this event. She tried her best but I lost her midway.

Riya: What do you mean by "she could not make it to this event"? Where is she now?

Avantika: I lost her just two weeks back. She was suffering from stomach cancer. The doctors tried their best to save her, but, alas, she left for her heavenly abode.

For a minute there was pin-drop silence in the air. The three friends were not ready to accept the fact that their lovely friend is not alive.

Sneha: But how come she was replying to all my queries on chats and e-mails? You are lying to us.

Avantika: That was me who was reverting on everything you all were asking my mom.

Sneha: But why were you doing this?

Common sense prevailed and Riya understood the whole situation.

Riya: That is why she was not taking my calls. Every time she would answer me via chats or e-mails only. She would always cut my calls and would reply with a standard remark, "I am busy somewhere" or "Will call you later." So, now I comprehend that it was you Avantika who made sure that we remain connected without creating any doubts in our minds.

Avantika: Yes Aunty. It was my mother's wish that you three come together to our coffee shop. She wanted that you all have a ball of a time. The plan of making you all wait for her was crafted by my mom. She did not want you all to mourn her loss at the very first meeting. My mom was a lively lady and loved you all very much. She wanted her to be remembered in the same way.

However hard the rest three pals tried to control their tears, at this point, it became impossible for them to balance their emotions. Their faces turned pale as if the mountain of sorrows had befallen their head. They all started crying inconsolably. Avantika tried her best to comfort them. Seeing the young girl soothing them, they realized how hard it would have been for the daughter to manage the entire episode. Moreover, Jolly wanted them to spend the day in a happy zone. Thus, they stopped sobbing after a while and then started sharing all the exciting stories of the days they had spent with her mother. A few instances incited a lot of laughter.

The next day, they all left for the institute that had been the seed of their friendship. Avantika accompanied them as she was too eager to see the same. Even her mother had asked her to go along with her old friends. They all cherished the golden days they had spent together on the campus of the college. All three went to every spot and revealed to Avantika the memories attached to it. The funny stories that cooked during the period, especially all anecdotes related to Jolly were shared with Avantika. The young girls thoroughly enjoyed those narratives. For her, this was going to be a lifetime memory.

It was becoming very hard to leave Avantika alone, but then they have to move on to their respective destination. At the departure time, they all sat with Avantika for one final goodbye.

Riya: I don't feel like leaving you here. Come with me to my home Avantika.

Avantika: I wanted to but I cannot as the running of these outlets needs my time and attention. Dad is not keeping too well and he is under depression after Mom's demise. I need to keep a check on him regularly.

Sneha: We can understand dear. Never feel isolated or lonely. We cannot fill the gap of your mother but whenever you want to share something that you would have liked to discuss with your mother, then feel free to call us. We would always have an ear for all your concerns.

Avantika: Thank you for your kind words.

Akansha: Ok, now come on, give us a big hug.

Saying this Akansha almost tried carrying the girl in her lap. One by one, they all caressed Avantika as if she were their child. The three friends **'Promised'** Avantika that they would be there for her whenever she requires their presence. They invited her to visit their houses whenever she feels like it.

Friendship is the purest relationship on earth. It is not bonded by the virtue of the warm blood flowing in your body. It is something that gets nurtured by a period of love, care, and affection.

!!!

Group

Who does not like to be a part of "The Group"? Except for a few who prefers a life of solitude. It takes time, effort, and patience to build a group, then remain part of it, and finally sustain it forever.

This story revolves around four friends, all possessing different attitudes, characters, and viewpoints on anything & everything.

Sudhir was the angry young chap and it was very easy to irritate him (but do that at your own risk). His father worked in the district municipality and his mother was a librarian in a private school. It was difficult to explain what made him fume all the time. With all the hotness from the outside, he also possessed a soft personality completely different from his livid image. He was pure by heart. Anything that he feels from inside would easily reflect on his face, so no hiding business, everything was crystal clear in his life. His fundamentals were very open, live and let others live.

Vaibhav was a mental, quite moody person whose actions and reactions could never be anticipated in advance. Nobody knew why he has become like that but everyone loved him. He never spoke ill of anyone and was able to mix in every type of group irrespective of whether it is the girl's mob or boy's gang in the class. His father worked in the central industrial security force and his mother was a homemaker.

Rohit was the naughtiest and chirpiest among all of them who planned all the silliest and wickedest activities in the group. The most sociable and easy-to-deal-with guy but quite sensitive. He was someone who could cry after watching an emotional movie or could feel the pain of a hungry puppy in the street. His father was a mechanical engineer in a government undertaking company and his mother was a housewife.

Tapas the last character was a straight and cool guy like an innocent holy cow. It was very difficult to pinpoint anything wrong with him, a good son, a good student, and a good friend. But to be frank his world lacked excitement, it was boring. He did not have any mission, vision, or statement in life which meant he was aimless and goalless. Both his parents were government servants who were working hard to make the life of their son comfortable.

They all under different circumstances came under a single roof and created a bond of a lifetime.

Tapas and Rohit were childhood friends but due to the sudden transfer of Tapas's father, he and his family had to shift to some other location. Sudhir was in the same school where Rohit studied but both never interacted with each other as they two were in different sections. Vaibhav was nowhere in the scene as his parents were in a different location altogether. Their story started once all four had passed their 10th board exam and reached standard 11th. Tapas's father got transferred back to the same town where Rohit and Sudhir were studying, so he put his son in the same school as theirs. Vaibhav's parents had newly shifted to the town and they too put him in the same school where the three boys had already enrolled for higher secondary studies. Sudhir, Tapas, Vaibhav, and Rohit were now together as all had taken science as their academic stream.

So on the first day of standard 11, all four boarded the same school bus, and in the very first meeting, Vaibhav and Sudhir had a massive fight. It so happened that Sudhir wanted to sit at the window aisle where Vaibhav was already seated. In the first instance, Sudhir requested Vaibhav to shift to some other place but on seeing his stubbornness, he started to abuse him which angered Vaibhav. He hit Sudhir in with all his energy in the face. This infuriated Sudhir and there was a full-blown bout between them. To meddle and stop the same, Rohit and Tapas had to intervene. As a result, they too had to suffer minor injuries. But this occurrence opened a gate for friendship among them. Rohit made sure that the situation gets lightened and no more tension flared between them. He invited the rest three pals into his house for a small get-together which enabled them to create a positive friendly bond among themselves.

###########################

One incident which was scary but finally turned into a funny scene was the "spirit call" they planned in one of the evenings (basically a process by which the soul of a dead person is being aroused). They had decided that they would ask a few questions about their concerns with the 'spirit'. It is believed that the soul of a dead person could foresee the future. There was a secluded place where they all gathered to perform the frightening trick. The role of each one was assigned after a general discussion among themselves. Sudhir was supposed to utter "Spirit calls" in a very low voice and Rohit was to follow the same with a remark "Please come." Vaibhav had to concentrate on the 'spirit' they wanted to call. It was decided by general consent of all that they would be calling the soul of "Sanjeev Kumar," one of the Bollywood legends who expired 25 years back. Tapas was overall in charge and he was managing the complete show.

They started with full vigor but somehow in the middle, the entire group began failing miserably. The reason was that every word uttered by both the friends Sudhir and Rohit was in a loud tone. The same was getting echoed in the room. Because of these, all three of them except Vaibhav could not control their laughter. Imagine "spirit call" resonating on multiple occasions and similarly "please come" rebounding several times. The event which was to be a completely sober and serious affair turned into a comedy show. Vaibhav was getting irritated as he was trying to focus on the spirit of the actor but the continuous hilarious reaction from his pal prevented him to do so. Finally, he lost his cool and gave one tight slap to Tapas (the reason why he chose Tapas is still unknown).

Tapas got furious and instead of reacting violently, he started vociferously abusing Vaibhav. For a few minutes, the situation became very tense but then they all started laughing as if they had consumed marijuana (a drug where one is not able to control their emotions). The episode made them comprehend very well that the group must not enter into a thoughtful zone as they are not good at it. Henceforth they avoided indulging in any serious activity.

##########################

One event which brought the entire group together was a petrifying journey that they all had to cover every day. The four friends got stuck in a very fearful situation. All of them used to go to tuition classes and the distance of the same was almost 10 kilometers from their houses. 8 kilometers they used to cover by private buses and the rest 2 kilometers was a thin forest area where they had to tread by walking. It was quite safe as the area was not part of the main forest (the main dense jungle was almost 5 kilometers away). But one fine day there was a rumor that a lion has been spotted in the location and just a day before, it has killed one of the calves. This created terror in the hearts of the four young minds. They were also excited as they knew that today they will have to coordinate differently so that they reach the final destination safely unscathed. They more or less worked like an army regiment, Sudhir took the initiative of covering by running the first 100 meters of the route ahead and then he whistled, indicating to the rest of his friends that the trip is safe, so they can cover the same. Each of the friends took turns in which they carefully covering 100 meters one by one and then asked the rest three to join subsequently. In this way, they roofed 2 kilometers in 20 minutes which generally takes 40 minutes to cover on a regular day. It was as if they are running for their life. They finally succeeded in the same. Tapas was the one who was very afraid initially but with the encouragement of his friends, he too got the courage and later the expedition became more fun.

For them, it was a mission accomplished and for the next week, they repeated the same activity. They also carried a thick stick and a few stones so that they could save themselves in case of an attack from wild animals. This incident brought teamwork to the group and they became closer to each other in terms of coordination and cooperation. It was also the most thrilling and enchanting experience of their life.

###########################

Their world rotated around school, a house, and a small playground where they used to play cricket. Sudhir was a pace bowler and Vaibhav was a good batsman. Tapas and Rohit were average on both parameters and adjusted as per the situation required. When the four of them grouped, they never needed anyone else to join them in the game. They were too satisfied among themselves and never felt the need for a better playground or a better ball or a better bat or a better companionship. The ground was almost adjoining Rohit's house, so gathering at the location for them was easier.

One evening when the boys had assembled at the place to play the game, it was Vaibhav who challenged Sudhir to give his best delivery and he promised that he would smash it off very hard. It was like instigating Sudhir who got ready to put his best foot forward. To deliver the best, he took a 50-meter-run, Vaibhav was holding his bat tightly as he too wanted to prove a point. Tapas and Rohit were quite amused as they were having complete fun watching the tense environment created between the two friends. While Rohit was boosting Sudhir, Tapas was motivating Vaibhav to give his best gunshot. Sudhir, finally bowled at a lightning speed, with one bounce, and Vaibhav with full force swung his bat with the momentum of thunder. Funnily, it did not hit the ball, rather the bat slipped from the hands of Vaibhav, flew atop, and landed on the asbestos sheet of Rohit's house. With a deafening noise, the bat hit the sheet and it broke into two pieces.

Rohit's father was having his evening tea when this incident occurred. The noise of the bang was so ear-piercing that he got a bit alarmed. He could not understand what has happened. This made him run outside to check and was startled to find the actual occurrence (he found boys were trying their best to hide). He grasped the situation and asked Rohit about it and out of fear he blurted out the entire narrative. Vaibhav had to face the burnt as Rohit's father scolded him for being so irresponsible.

The result was that for next the ten days Vaibhav was nowhere to be seen. He could not muster enough courage to come back to the ground even though Rohit tried convincing him his best. The rest three friends had a laugh riot getting to know how his daring friend is now terrified to even come back to play.

######################

There is one more story that created a ripple in their lives. Vaibhav was a very temperamental guy and it was never easy to understand what is going on in his mind. Rather everyone would remain on their toes guessing as to how would he react in a particular situation. One such incident where he acted beyond anyone's imagination was when the results of the 12th pre-board exams were declared. Most of the students had failed in at least 2 or 3 subjects and the same was the case with Vaibhav. He had red marks in Physics and Chemistry. The questions were intentionally set tough by teachers as they wanted to give a warning to all of them that they cannot remain complacent while preparing for board final papers.

A maximum of the students took it in a positive stride but Vaibhav as usual took it in another way. Rather he ran away from school as he was not able to handle the pressure of being a failure. The baggage of non-achievement was too much for him. When the news reached his parent's ears, they had a nervous breakdown but with the support of friends and relatives, gathered themselves up and filed a missing complaint at the local police station. The hunt for the boy started immediately in all directions. The local authorities also took the help of three friends in understanding all possibilities and probabilities of the location to where he could have escaped. The three pals were worried as this was something they had least anticipated.

Finally, the police made a breakthrough and he was found crossing the border of the state with the help of a truck driver who had given him a lift. They did that with the understanding that the child wants to reach his home which is across the border (This is what Vaibhav has explained to the motorist). Nobody enquired a single question of him, nor was he asked to justify the reason for eloping as all wanted him to relax first and these questions could be taken later with him. Sudhir, Rohit, and Tapas made sure that nobody makes fun of their friend in school or the locality. They stood their ground in favor of him by restricting anyone who tried to question him about the incident. It's a different thing that after some time all four gossiped about this incident amongst themselves with lots and lots of laughter pulling each other legs, especially the hero of the episode, mental Vaibhav.

#########################

One more incident which brought all four friends to bond was the sudden sweet love affair of Tapas. He was a very soft-spoken boy in the class and every girl liked him for his courteous nature. There was one girl named Swati with whom Tapas had a fascination. He had openly discussed this with all his friends as to how much he adores this girl. She also had mutual feelings for Tapas. The love story of the couple was running smoothly but then faced an obstacle due to a villain in the story named Vikram. All four friends were from the science stream including the girl Swati, whereas Vikram was from the Arts section.

Vikram too liked Swati, and on a few occasions tried to tease her. One day when she could not take it any longer, she spoke about it to Tapas. Simultaneously he informed all of his three friends about the same. All four went to the boy to explain to him in a very decent manner that he should not do all these cheap vulgar acts. If she does not like you, then back off immediately. But Vikram continued his unrefined ways of creating problems for the girl.

This angered the group and one day all four friends thrashed the boy very badly. Though he too was not alone, the group of four friends was a force to reckon with. Vikram's friends did not have a chance, as the group of four friends overpowered his disoriented pals.

Seeing that it is impossible to hold ground against the four friends, Vikram finally backed off. This incident brought a lot of unity to their friendship. They pledged that they would stand with each other, however odd or tough the situation is.

####################

Rohit and Tapas shared a special bond as they knew each other since standard 3 as mentioned earlier in the story. It so happened that just before the 12th board exam, Rohit's grandmother expired due to old age. He was heartbroken as he loved his grandmamma a lot but then as his exams were near, he had to pay full attention to his studies. Lots of relatives stayed back in his home for the thirteen days ritual, so for test preparation, he used to go to Tapas's house. Tapas's father and mother were working professionals, so he remained all alone in the home. Thus, both friends used to do joint studies. Tapas had lots of decent solved test papers, especially one of the books on chemistry subject which he had borrowed from a teacher. The organic and inorganic part was explained in a very crispy and precise manner.

Well both the friends had a good time reading together as they would clarify each other's doubts through combined study. Rohit would usually jot down all important and relevant points from the manuscript for revision back at home. He was quite confident about the rest of the subjects as he had been rereading all the relevant topics multiple times. He believed in his hard work but for chemistry, in a way, he had become dependent on Tapas.

Tapas, on the other hand, was a very sweet friend and on several occasions, he would lend his books to his friend. Tapas's parents were happy that both the boys are studying rigorously together. Rohit had a reputation for being a very sincere person in academics.

Very soon the exams approached and all four friends gave their best. This is what was expected of them as being laborious is within your limit, but the result is beyond one's control.

On vacation, they had a lovely time, enjoying, playing, and spending time with friends and family. After two months, the results were supposed to come out. Rohit was confident in all the subjects except Chemistry as most of the study he did was based on the joint study and the book that Tapas shared with him. On the other hand, Tapas was confident in Chemistry (for the rest of the paper, he was quite unsure).

On the day the marks were supposed to come out, all four friends took the blessings of their parents, prayed to God, and left for school. The marks were displayed on the school notice board and all the friends were curious to know the outcome. Vaibhav and Sudhir took the lead as they were the tallest in the group and as the board was surrounded by lots of students, their height played an important part in extracting the results from the notification panel. Both standing behind could gauge the result owing to their extraordinary tallness. Their eyes twinkled when they saw the results as out of 40 students Rohit was 2nd ranker, Tapas 9th, Vaibhav 13th and Sudhir 18th. Both announced the results loudly and hugged each other, rather all four started dancing out of joy. There was just one curiosity, which was the mark in Chemistry as both Tapas and Rohit had an eye on it. Rohit had scored better than Tapas. For a minute Tapas could not believe it as he expected that he would outscore Rohit at least in one subject. For some time, he remained sad but then he controlled his emotions and congratulated his friend on the achievement.

Sometimes you become a medium for others' success, which is completely ok. Everyone has a different journey.

######################

After board exams, all four friends left for different technical lines, and the communication between them almost got halted for a long period. Vaibhav joined an IT firm in Malaysia, Sudhir started working at a knowledge process outsourcing company, Tapas in a pharma company and Rohit became a hotelier. Who would have imagined that these four friends would join a unique line which is entirely different from each other? The crux of the situation was that it has been 5 straight years and none of them were in contact with each other.

As usual, Rohit took the initiative and collected the mobile numbers of all his old friends from different resources. Once in touch, he planned for an out-and-out tour of any fun beach in the country. All four friends promised that they would surely be part of it. Keeping their pledges alive, all the pals joined Goa for a grand get-together.

It was a trip to remember as they knew that this could be the last meet when they all gathered collectively at a destination (so they made the most of it). It was a three-night trip and they partied hard, sang, danced, and remembered the good old days. Lots of pictures and videos were clicked which they posted on different social media to keep the memories alive. Between them, nothing has changed, nobody talked about their current job, no one discussed the package they are earning currently, and not a single conversation on the properties they have or are planning to erect, the only thing that they deliberated was the good old days of childhood. They discussed how badly they miss the golden period of their life, that is the days they spent together. Reminiscing, of the fabulous old period which was free of tensions, strains, and pressures.